THE NOTEBOOKS OF ANDRÉ WALTER

André Gide

THE
NOTEBOOKS
OF ANDRÉ WALTER

*Translated from the French
and with an Introduction and Notes
by Wade Baskin*

PHILOSOPHICAL LIBRARY

New York

Library of Congress Catalog Card No. 67-24573

Printed in Great Britain for Philosophical Library

ISBN 978-0-8065-3022-7

CONTENTS

INTRODUCTION

Publication of *The Notebooks of André Walter* early in 1891 marked the formal entrance of André Gide (1869-1951) into the literary world of Paris. He had thought that his message would bring him lasting fame. With funds provided by his mother, he had planned to publish two editions of the *Notebooks*: a limited *de luxe* edition for his friends and a large plain edition for the public. The plain edition, containing the sub-title *œuvre posthume* but not the author's name, appeared first. Gide's confidence was severely shaken when, instead of creating the sensation he had envisioned, the work was unenthusiastically received. He salvaged a few copies, keeping some for himself and selling the rest for scrap. Still, this first rebuff was not catastrophic, for the *Notebooks* set a pattern which persisted through the years and formed the substructure of the master-works of his maturity: the search for catharsis and liberation through literary creation. Years after their abortive publication, in *If It Die* (1926) Gide wrote: 'It was not only my first work, it was my summation.'

His first sustained prose work is more than a painful analysis of the inner conflicts of a sensitive adolescent. It is a prefiguration of the direction of Gide's subsequent development as a man and as an artist. Each of his works may be viewed as a milestone in his quest for authenticity, an experiment in self-analysis through the medium of art. He once complained that La Bruyère painted men as they were, but without telling us how they became what they were. In the *Notebooks* Gide tries to overcome this de-

7

ficiency by projecting on the printed page the inner conflicts of André Walter, his ill-starred double. Here, in the first of a long series of semi-autobiographical studies in the tradition of Montaigne and Pascal, Gide tries to harmonize the warring elements in his own nature.

He has suggested that the conflicting elements in his nature are traceable to the duality of his background and to early childhood experiences. While he probably exaggerated the importance of heredity in trying to explain the conflicts which motivated the development of his major themes, he was the product of two cultures—Catholic Normandy and Huguenot Uzès in the south of France. His father, Paul Gide, was born in the small town of Uzès, near Nîmes, in Languedoc. Paul Gide married Juliette Rondeaux in 1863 and lived with her in Paris, where he was professor of Roman Law, until his death in 1880. Juliette Rondeaux came from a family that had lived in Rouen for five generations. Originally of peasant Catholic stock, the family had prospered and Juliette's grandparents had embraced Protestantism. According to Gide, it was his mother who awakened his moral conscience and his father who revealed to him the world of art. His childhood was strongly influenced by his mother's piety, her strong sense of duty, and her condemnation of sensual indulgence, all of which led Henri Peyre to speak of her 'loving tyranny'.

The crucial incident of Gide's youth is the one analysed in the *Notebooks*: the awakening of his love for Madeleine Rondeaux. He had suffered since early childhood from nervous tension, excessive timidity and feelings of inferiority. He began to practise self-abuse at an early age and was expelled from school, at the age of eight, when this habit was discovered. Loneliness, unnamed fears and nightmares caused him intense suffering during his sombre childhood. Then Madeleine, his cousin, entered his life. Two years older than he, she nevertheless represented innocence, purity and moral perfection. She appears as Emmanuèle ('God with us') in the *Notebooks* and under various names in his other works. With characteristic candour Gide recorded in his memoirs the events leading to the communion of thoughts and ideas experienced by these two suffering, frightened children. She was fourteen and he was twelve when one day he entered her room unexpectedly, to find her on her knees. He kissed her, whereupon he noticed that her cheeks were wet with tears. She confided that she had learned of her mother's secret love affair, and he felt that the shock of her discovery—which she was forced to withhold from all others, including her father whom she idolized—would mark her for life. Awareness of her need for him gave him a purpose, an ideal. The desire to comfort and protect Madeleine elevated him and inspired in him a mystical love, which coincided with the awakening of his literary vocation.

Gide belongs to a generation of writers who were not afraid to experiment with traditional art forms. Each of his writings stresses his freedom as an artist. Given certain materials, he tries to weave them into an artistic expression of some profound human experience. The tortured history of his adolescence, his temptations and anguish, his guilt and, hopefully, his eventual triumph over demoniac forces through his love for Madeleine are the raw elements of the *Notebooks*. The work was to be more than a unique revelation of the universality of suffering and despair; it was to be a noble, moving declaration of his unsullied love for Madeleine and a manifesto written for an expectant audience. He had determined at the age of sixteen to complete the great manifesto, in which he intended to lay bare the inmost secrets of the human heart, before his twentieth year. First, however, he had to complete his studies and prepare himself for his task.

He began to keep a journal, hoping to use this material in his great work. He felt that the crisis in his own life would provide a framework for his book, and the first emotional upheaval in his life seems also to have been the most significant from the aesthetic viewpoint. His love for Madeleine was so pure and mystical that he was never able to associate it with ordinary physical love. His intimacy with his cousin made everything in his life take on new meaning. They spent many hours together, sharing their thoughts and reading the works of poets and thinkers—Verlaine, Baudelaire, Goethe, the Greek poets. Their preferred language was the language of religious aspiration. Typical is the passage transcribed from his journal and attributed to André Walter in the *Notebooks*: 'We are alone in your room, overcome by tenderness and passion. In the caress of the air . . . something ineffable causes tears to flow and the soul to escape from the body and to coalesce in an embrace.'

It is not unusual for a first love to evoke feelings of mystical or religious exaltation that seem to banish sensual desires, but in the normal course of events these conflicting elements are harmonized. In Gide's case a sense of guilt was aroused by his failure to live according to the strict moral code prescribed by his mother and later by Madeleine, by his obsession with carnality in the form of onanism. Sex and sin were intimately fused in his thoughts. The weight of the flesh, which checked his aspiration towards Madeleine and God, could be transcended only by his primary vision.

One summer he decided to travel through Brittany alone (even though his mother insisted on meeting him at fixed points) and to keep a diary during his tour. His first writings were an experiment in rhythm. Titled 'Reflections from Elsewhere—Minor Studies in Rhythm', they were published in the literary review *Wallonie* under the signature 'André Walter'.

He had now taken a first step towards the realization of his project. Back in Paris in the autumn of 1889, he passed the baccalaureate examinations which he had failed in July. He studied with a former professor, read Schopenhauer's *The World as Will and Idea* and Bergson's *Essay on the Immediate Data of Consciousness*, and met frequently with Pierre Louis. He had met Pierre Louis at the Ecole Alsacienne, where they were rivals for first place in their literature class. They shared a love for literature and the arts, and they made plans for founding a literary review.

By spring Gide felt that the time had come to finish his project. Convinced that he must find complete seclusion in order to do what he had to do, he moved into a chalet not far from the famed Carthusian monastery near Grenoble in south-eastern France. There, on the shores of Lake Annecy, surrounded by orchards and with only a piano as his companion, he set to work and allowed nothing to interfere with his schedule of writing.

He first envisioned his work as inconsecutive, plotless, melancholy and romantic, metaphysical and profound. At the time of the publication of the *Notebooks*, Gide told Valéry in a letter that he had drawn on 'Mallarmé for poetry, Maeterlinck for drama—myself for the novel'.

His task was nothing less than that of reshaping the current forms of the novel, and his approach to the novel was supposedly as revolutionary as Mallarmé's approach to poetry and Maeterlinck's to drama. Gide's plans were modified during the composition of the *Notebooks*, however, when he began to fear that his book would contain 'empty declamation', and he decided to include the fictionalized account of his love for Madeleine. He had resolved to marry his cousin as soon as possible, notwithstanding the opposition of his mother and Madeleine. His book was to be a lover's gambit as well as a bid for glory.

The narrative of the book closely parallels the relationship between André Gide and Madeleine Rondeaux. In the opening section of the first notebook, *The White Notebook*, André Walter lyrically addresses his soul, which once again has succumbed to sin : 'Wait till your sadness is assuaged, poor soul, wearied by the struggle of yesterday . . . cherished hopes will blossom anew.' For the life of action he has only scorn : 'Nothing happens. Always the quiet life—and yet a turbulent life. Everything happens deep in the soul. Nothing appears on the surface.' In recounting the story of André Walter's love for Emmanuèle, Gide quotes liberally from his own journal, the Bible, Goethe, and Amiel, whose *Journal intime* is itself a masterpiece of self-analysis and a fascinating mirror of a sensitive mind struggling to fashion a set of values in an age marked by growing scepticism and pessimism.

In *The White Notebook*, which seems to be a condemnation of ordinary conjugal love, Emmanuèle is idealized to the point of being divested of her physical nature. André Walter realizes that he can never marry Emmanuèle, that his passion can never be satisfied in life, but that he can possess her spiritually after her death. The loosely-knit recapitulation of his metaphysical anguish, his literary problems, and his struggles for purity reveals his preference for unsatisfied passion over consummated love (the Tristan legend), his acceptance of the fundamental cleavage between soul (the Manichean principle of good) and body (the Manichean principle of evil), and his conviction that 'love transcends mourning and death'.

In the last pages of *The White Notebook* André Walter recalls his mother's final decree : Emmanuèle must marry another. The decree was carried out as soon as the period of mourning ended. André Gide, who had manifested an ambivalent feeling towards his mother through the years, had not yet asked Madeleine to marry him. Mme Gide had advised him not to marry his cousin; apart from the fact that they were closely related, she felt that her son was too immature and too irresponsible to care for Madeleine. Though older than he, Madeleine needed a sense of stability and security which he could not provide. The youth nevertheless charged his mother with interfering with his plans and continued his suit. The bedside scene in which André Walter renounces possession of Emmanuèle in favour of a higher union anticipates the relationship supposedly maintained by André Gide after his unconsummated marriage to Madeleine Rondeaux, whom he later referred to as 'the only love in my life'.

André Walter's march to disaster is charted in the second section, *The Black Notebook*, which opens on an elegiac note: 'My soul sings . . . so that you may know at last how enduring was our love.' André Walter writes at once the story of his own life and that of his fictional creation, Allain, sometimes dividing the pages in order to present both narratives concurrently. The demoniac forces which threaten to destroy the writer cannot be exorcized in the manner prescribed by Faust, whose words (*Sei ruhig Pudel! renne nicht hin und wieder!*) are quoted early in the section. He succumbs time after time to the fantasies of onanism and is driven to the verge of madness by feelings of guilt and remorse. *The Black Notebook* becomes a race to determine who will lose his sanity first. Allain's epitaph has already been written: 'Here lies Allain who became mad because he thought he had a soul.' A short time later his creator falls victim to 'brain fever', the malady prized by nineteenth-century romanticists, and writes his last words: 'How good it would be to sleep there . . . . The snow is pure.'

Gide completed his first novel by July of 1890—before the end of his twentieth year. In a few special copies of the *Notebooks*, the name Madeleine was substituted for Emmanuèle. Gide gave her a copy with an appropriate inscription and asked her to read it immediately. Her diary shows that she was moved to tears when she finally read it, but she found it too true to life and considered it to be an invasion of her privacy. Her polite but formal rejection of his proposal hurt him deeply. In 1895, however, shortly after the death of his mother, André Gide and Madeleine Rondeaux were married.

Though his first work was a commercial failure, it was praised by other writers. Stéphane Mallarmé and Henri de Régnier praised the delicate quality of its style. Maurice Maeterlinck said that it 'eternalized' the struggles of a virtuous soul. Joris-Karl Huysmans saw in André Walter's plight a new 'sickness of the century'. Rémy de Goncourt hailed the book as the distillation of all the study, dreaming, passion and anguish associated with youth; he called the unknown author of the *Notebooks* a romantic-philosophical disciple of Goethe.

As Harold March states in *Gide and the Hound of Heaven* (1952): 'All of the Gide to come is implicit in the *Cahiers*, which in its very confusion is more revealing than the chastened art of his maturity.' In this deliberately chaotic work, we see Gide 'struggling to escape from the labyrinth of his obsessions—upward towards God, outward towards nature and his fellow creatures'. André Walter, the first typical Gidean hero, enables Gide to conduct a rewarding dialogue with the reader. He reminds us that every writer of fiction constructs an imaginary world in order to gain access to the real world. Here as in the great works of his maturity, he raises more questions than he answers. In the words of Germaine Brée and Margaret Guiton (*The French Novel*, 1957), he refuses to 'let us sit back comfortably and enjoy his novel'. 'I am telling you a story,' he reminds us with gentle irony. 'What do you make of it?'

In preparing the Introduction and Notes to my translation of *Les Cahiers d'André Walter* I have drawn freely from the writings of Germaine Brée, Jean Delay, Wallace Fowlie, Jean Hytier and Harold March. I wish also to express my appreciation to all those who have helped me to prepare this edition of Gide's first substantive work for publication : Mr Ralph Behrens, who read the first draft of *The White Notebook*; Miss Mildred Riling, who criticized the first draft of *The Black Notebook*; Mr Jim Barnes, Mr James Coe, Mrs Joann Freeman, Mme Nicole Hatfield and Miss Brenda Lane, who helped with the translation; and Mrs Vlasta Baskin, Miss Judy Bauer, Mrs Mary Frye and Mr William McCray, who helped to prepare the typescript.

Southeastern State College   W.B.

15

THE WHITE NOTEBOOK

WAIT TILL your sadness is assuaged, poor soul, wearied by the struggle of yesterday.

Wait.

When tears are shed
cherished hopes will blossom anew.
Now you must sleep.

Lullabies, ballads, barcaroles,
The song of the willows smoothes the cadence.

You must say a good prayer this evening, and you must believe. This you will have for ever. No one can take it from you. You will say : *'The Lord is the portion of mine inheritance . . . when my father and my mother forsake me, then the Lord will take me up.'*[1]
And then you will sleep. Think no more; bitter days are still too near.
Let memories feed your dreams.
Rest.

[1] Gide rightly emphasized in many of his writings the influence of his early puritanical training on his art. According to him, two-thirds of the biblical quotations set down in the first draft of the *Notebooks* were eliminated before publication at the suggestion of his friend, Albert Démarest.

Thursday

Wrote some letters . . . .

I tried to read, to think . . . . Exhaustion soothed my sadness, which now seems but a dream.

Now beneath the trees
The darkness is comforting.

How silent is the night. I am almost afraid to fall asleep. I am alone. Thought emerges from a dark background; the future appears above the dark as a ribbon of space. Nothing distracts me from *my primary vision*. I am this vision and nothing more.[2]

Some evening, turning back, I shall repeat these words of sorrow; now it sickens me to write. Words are not for these things, not for emotions too pure to be spoken. I am afraid that empty, high-sounding words are blasphemous; hating the words that I have loved too much, I wish to write badly by design. I wish to disrupt harmonies wherever they happen to exist.[3]

Rest in peace, Mother. I have been obedient.

My soul still smarts from its dual ordeal, but sadness is giving way to pride of conquest. You knew me well if you thought that by its very excess virtue would entice me. You knew that arduous and challenging paths lure me, that senseless pursuits appeal to me because of my dream, and that a little folly is necessary for the satisfaction of my pride.[4]

[2] The primary vision (*la vision commencée*) appears in *Urien's Voyage* as the idea or principle which each of us is to manifest in his own life. This section reflects the influence of Schopenhauer's *The World as Will and Idea* on the young writer.

[3] In a later preface to the *Notebooks* (1930), the author expressed regret over its defects, holding that the writer should always exercise absolute control over his medium.

[4] Gide later condemned the pride that resulted from such a victory. He insisted that he had at first thought it good to struggle, that true wisdom consisted in accepting defeat, in not opposing oneself.

You made them all depart in order that you might speak to me alone (it was only a few hours before the end).

'André my child,' you said, 'I want to die assured.'

I already knew what you would say to me and had summoned up all my strength. You hastened to speak because you were very tired.

'It would be good for you to leave Emmanuèle . . . . Your affection is fraternal—make no mistake about it . . . . It springs from the life in common that you have been leading. Although she is my niece, do not make me regret having treated her as my own since she became an orphan. I would not wish to allow you complete freedom, for fear that your emotions would mislead you and make the both of you unhappy. Do you understand why? Emmanuèle has already suffered much. I want more than anything else for her to be happy. Do you love her enough to prefer her happiness to yours?'[5]

Then you spoke of T*** who had just responded to the sad news.

'Emmanuèle thinks highly of him,' you remarked.

I knew that she did, but I remained silent.

'Have I put too much trust in you, my child?' you continued, 'Or can I die assured?'

I was exhausted by the recent ordeals.

'Yes, Mother,' I said, not really understanding but wishing to continue to the end—to hurl myself into the heart of darkness.

I departed. When they summoned me, I saw Emmanuèle near your bed, clasping the hand of T***. We knelt and prayed. My thoughts were confused—then you went to sleep.

After the palliative rites, we had communion together.

---

[5] Jean Delay in his monumental work on the early life of Gide (*La Jeunesse d'André Gide,* Gallimard, 1956) maintains that in the foregoing passage the writer reveals for the first time one of the deepest secrets of his psychology: the influence of his mother in preventing his physical union with Madeleine Rondeaux.

The White Notebook

Emmanuèle was in front of me. I did not look at her. To avoid thinking of her and lapsing into reveries, I repeated: 'Since I must lose her, may I at least find Thee again, O Lord. Bless me for following the strait and narrow path.'

Then I departed. I came here because I could not rest.[6]

Thursday

I worked in order to keep my mind occupied. It is through work that my mind is revitalized.

I took out all the written pages which recall the past. I want to read them once more, to arrange them, to copy them, to relive them. I will write some stories based on old memories.

I will turn my thoughts from earlier dreams in order to begin a new life. When memories are set down, my soul will be lighter.[7] I will stop them in their flight. Whatever is not yet forgotten is not entirely dead. I do not wish to leave behind me without even a parting nod the enduring fancies of my youth.

But why try to find reasons to justify a stand already taken, as if by way of an apology? I write because I need to write—and that sums up everything. A stand is weakened by attempted explanations; the act should be spontaneous.

And with revitalized ambition comes a reawakening of the hope of completing *Allain*, the book that I have long dreamed of writing.[8]

[6] Publication of the *Notebooks* did mark a turning point in the life of the author. It marked the end of his sheltered life of mystic reverie and passive introspection and the beginning of an active life of exploration and conquest. Schopenhauer's visionary became the romantic disciple of Goethe.

[7] Setting the pattern that was to serve for a lifetime of creative effort, the author abstracts from reality and freely changes details. His mother's words might well have been spoken after the death of Emile Rondeaux, the father of Madeleine (Emmanuèle).

[8] It is significant that the book originally envisioned as *Allain* was finally published as *The Notebooks of André Walter*. The German name suggests of course Goethe's *Werther*, which has a similar theme and which Gide was reading during the period of the composition of the *Notebooks*.

20th April

The air is so radiant this morning that in spite of myself my soul hopes—and sings, and worships prayerfully.

> *E però leva su! Vince l'ambascia*
> *Con l'animo che vince ogni battaglia*
> *Se col suo grave corpo non s'accascia . . .*
> *E dissi: 'Va, ch'i son forte e ardito' . . . .*[9]

21st April

Nothing happens. Always the quiet life—and yet such a turbulent life. Everything happens deep in the soul. Nothing appears on the surface. How can I write about nothing? My thoughts have nothing on which to build, and my persistent passions, offspring of a forgotten past, have imperceptibly reached their peak.[10]

I would fashion a soul, shape it deliberately—a loving soul,

[9] And therefore raise thee up, o'ercome thy panting
With spirit that o'ercometh every battle,
If with its heavy body it sink not . . . .
And said: 'Go on, for I am strong and bold.'
(Longfellow's translation)

[10] The tumultuous inner life with its conflicting passions and ideals is an appropriate theme for Gide's first published work. During the period of its composition he expressed the opinion that the crisis depicted in it was of such general interest that others might use it before he completed his work. Later, in his autobiographical *If It Die* (1926), he wrote, 'It was not only my first book, it was my summation.'

[11] It has been said that Gide's art is a sustained attempt to understand and explain himself. Perhaps *The White Notebook* is a symbolic account of his struggle to free himself from carnal temptations through the mystic, idealized love first experienced in his youth. Delay sees the perfect image which he creates here (an Echo for Narcissus) as the projection of his superego: the embodiment in his love of all those qualities which he holds in high esteem. Jean-Paul Sartre's handling of a similar theme in *Saint-Genêt* (1952) suggests the connection between André Walter's search for a kindred soul and André Gide's predicament.

a beloved soul, similar to my own—in order that it might understand and yet from such a distance that nothing could ever separate the two. Slowly I would tie such intricate knots, weave such a network of sympathetic bonds, that separation would be impossible and shared patterns would for ever keep them side by side.[11]

Monday

We learned everything together. I thought only of joys shared with you, and you took pleasure in following my lead. Your vagabond mind also sought companionship.

First came the Greeks, always our favourites: the *Iliad*, *Prometheus*, *Agamemnon*, *Hippolytus*. And when, knowing the meaning, you wanted to hear the harmony of the lines, I would read:

> .... Τενέδοιό τε ἶφι ἀνάσσεις
> Σμινθεῦ............
> Τέχνον, τί χλαίεις; τίδέ σε φρένας ἵχετο πένθος;
> Αἵρετέ μου δέμας, ὀρθοῦτε χάρα.
> λέλυμαι μελέων σύνδεσμα, φίλαι.
> Αἴ, Αἴ,
> πῶς ἂν δροσερὰς ἀπό χρηνίδος
> χαθαρῶν, ὑδάτων πῶμ' ἀρυσαίμην......

Then came *King Lear*:
Through the sharp hawthorne blows the cold wind . . . .
Shakespeare's dramatic genius fired us with enthusiasm. There were no such thrills in real life.

Words of a Believer had the ring of true prophecy. Later, of course, you found Lamennais's eloquence somewhat trite. I was vexed by your criticism, even though apt, because emotion floods his pages, and emotion is always beautiful.

Then we would go back to childhood readings, first studied in

23

the classical manner with ravishing delight : Pascal, Bossuet . . .[12] Massillon. But instead of the specious charm of the *Carême* we preferred the word-magic of the *Funeral Orations* of Jansenist sternness . . . .

And so many others still—and all the others.

Acknowledging our common aspirations, we went on to Vigny, Baudelaire—to Flaubert, the friend long anticipated ![13] We marvelled at his masterful rhythm. The rhetorical subtleties of the Goncourts sharpened our minds; Stendhal made them more receptive, more critical . . . .[14]

ΣΥΜΠΑΘΕΙΝ: to suffer together, to be impassioned together.

I saw the Sphinx as it fled towards Libya; like a jackal it galloped along.

Loudly I declaimed it, developing first the line and then emphasizing the dactyl. Both of us trembled to the majestic cadences.

You wrote that T*** reread to us the other evening Du Camp and Flaubert's *Eastern Voyage.* He recited for us the rhythmical apostrophe that we love, but whether he reads it for us or I read it myself, the voice that I hear is always yours.

---

[12] Name crossed out. (Gide's note.)

[13] The notebooks in which Gide recorded his readings show that he read the writers mentioned here during the period of the composition of *The White Notebook*. Gustave Flaubert deserves special mention since he influenced Gide's aesthetics and caused him to consider titling his first book *The New Sentimental Education*. (Flaubert's *Sentimental Education* was inspired in part by personal reminiscences, notably those of his unhappy love affair, at sixteen, with an older woman who later lost her mind.)

[14] Word missing. (Gide's note.)

We were still reading from the *Temptation* :[15]

> *O Fantasy, bear me away on your wings to mitigate my*
> *sorrow . . . Egypt! Egypt! The shoulders of your great*
> *motionless Gods have been bleached by bird-droppings,*
> *and the wind that passes over the desert stirs the ashes of*
> *your dead! . . . Spring will return no more, O eternal*
> *Mother!*
> *. . . You cannot imagine the long journey that we have*
> *taken. The green courier's onagers died of exhaustion . . . .*

And we read much more until finally we tired of repeating
the passages, of bringing out all their harmony, of letting the
pulsating rhythms echo back and forth until the refrain clung
to the lips of one of us and was intelligible to the other—in the
absence of speech.

I related to you my aspirations; you smiled, trying your best
to seem incredulous.

'And the book that I have been dreaming of writing,' I told
you, 'will be called ALLAIN.'

Allain, the book that I dreamed of writing! I saw it as a
melancholy and romantic work at first, when with the stirring
of my senses I roamed the forests in search of solitude and was
prey to unknown anxieties; when the song of the wind in the
swaying pines seemed to give voice to my resurgent yearnings;
when I wept over falling leaves, over setting suns, over vanishing
streams of water; and when at the sound of the sea I would
lapse into a day of reverie. Then I saw it as metaphysical and

---

[15] *The Temptation of Saint Anthony*, a romantic adaptation of an old
Christian legend, pictures the hermit in the desert, tempted by sensual
pleasures and secret intellectual delights but victorious in his struggle to
remain virtuous.

profound when my mind began to harbour doubts—childish doubts, perhaps, but doubts that caused me considerable anxiety. There cannot be two ways of doubting.[16]

At the outset I saw the book as a character sketch with neither episodes nor plot.

Then I had the notion of studying our love rather than portraying a character who declaimed about such things, and of recreating the intensity and immediacy of our experience.[17]

25th April

They will never understand this book, those who search for happiness. The soul remains unsatisfied; it falls asleep amid happy surroundings. It becomes inert rather than alert. The soul should remain alert, active. It should find happiness not in HAPPINESS but in the awareness of its violent activity.

It follows that sorrow is to be preferred over joy, for it quickens the soul; when it does not vanquish it stimulates. It causes suffering, but pride of undaunted living compensates for minor lapses. Supreme arrogance is the mark of intense living. I would not exchange the intense life for any other; I have lived several lives, and the least of these was the real one.[18]

My life will be more intense, my soul more vigilant. My listless soul will no longer lament but will rejoice in its nobility.

[16] Gide wrote that Schopenhauer was responsible for his alternating periods of anguish and ecstasy, for his awareness of a second reality behind the visible one, and for his passion for poetry and music.

[17] Pierre Louis warned Gide against undertaking an autobiographical work at the age of twenty and cited Goethe's regret over the shortcomings of *Werther* as proof that such an undertaking should come towards middle age. Ironically, structural integrity and variety of detail, the two elements advocated by Louis, are missing from the *Notebooks*.

[18] This passage invites comparison of André Walter and his feminine counterpart, Alissa, in *Strait Is the Gate* (1909). She epitomizes the same ideal and mystical love. Afraid of physical love, she longs for an impossible happiness, for perfect Love, for God.

The thrill, both moral and physical, that grips you at the sight of sublime things, the thrill at first considered unique by each of us with the result that neither mentioned it to the other —what joy when we discovered that it was the same in both of us! It was an overwhelming emotion. What joy, afterwards, to experience it together as we read; it seemed to unite us in the same surge of enthusiasm. And the same thrill was soon felt by each of us through the other, in the other; with our hands joined and our bodies in close contact, we became inseparably one.

And when we read and my voice alternately rose and fell, I knew the sounds and the passages which we loved and which would make us both quiver with delight.

Fools! Nor would you have believed me . . .
Scamander, Meander, beloved of the Priamides.

The names alone, the Greek names with their long endings, awakened in us such magnificent memories that each burst of sound aroused latent feelings of exaltation.

One summer evening we were returning from H***. We had been left alone on top of the carriage. The others were inside. The route was long and night was coming on rapidly. We wrapped around us a common shawl; our cheeks almost touched.

'I have brought along the Gospel,' I said to her. 'If you wish, we can read together while there is still some light.'

'Read,' said Emmanuèle.[19]

---

[19] Emmanuèle is the fictional name of Madeleine Rondeaux, who appears under a different name in many other works. Significant details of her life before and after she became Mme André Gide have been related in subsequent works, notably *If It Die, Strait Is the Gate* and *Et nunc manet in te* (1951). These include the infidelity and divorce of her mother, the death of her father, and her unconsummated marriage together with the suffering, privation and shame which she endured for her husband's sake. In Gide's imagination Emmanuèle was transformed, idealized, ennobled, imbued with the very qualities he would like to have attributed to himself.

After I had finished reading to her, I asked : 'Shall we pray together?'

'No,' she answered. 'Let's pray silently. Otherwise we would think of ourselves rather than of God.'

We fell silent, but I was still thinking about you.

Night had fallen. 'What are you thinking about?' she asked. And I recited :

Friendly dawn sleeps in the valley . . . .

Then it was her turn :

> *Farewell, leisurely voyages, sounds heard from afar.*
> *Laughter of the passer-by, screeching of axle-tree,*
> *Unexpected turns along irregular slopes,*
> *A friend rediscovered, hours whiled away,*
> *Hope of arriving late in some wilderness* . . . .

Then mine again :

> *But you, indolent traveller, will you not*
> *Put your head on my shoulder and dream?*

And because it was growing late, both of us fell asleep, lost in dreams, our bodies in close contact, our hands joined . . . .

. . . Then suddenly a brutal awakening as if from a dream : we had run into a wagon on the dark road. We heard voices and the rattling of chains but saw nothing. We heard the barking of dogs and noticed a faint light outlined against the panes of a nearby farmhouse—or so we thought. Trembling a little, we drew even closer to each other, put our trust in each other.

> *Dreaming of black, heavy wagons that noisily by night*
> *Pass by the thresholds of farms*
> *And cause the dogs to bark in the dark.*

While we slept the lanterns had been lighted. We watched with amusement for the indistinct shapes of bushes to leap from the shadows as we passed by. We looked for known shapes which would tell us how far we had to travel.

Then the sound of footsteps : a belated traveller suddenly illuminated by a gust of light. And as the rays moved on through the darkness they silhouetted the shadows of night butterflies as they approached and collided with the panes in the lanterns.

I recall the warmer air that caressed our brows as we crossed empty fields and smelled the perfume of damp ploughed ground. We listened to the singing of the frogs . . . .

Then at last the arrival, laughter once again, the hearth, the lamp and warmth-giving tea. But both of us kept in our souls the memory of a deeper intimacy.

Not the landscape itself, not the emotion caused by the landscape. The setting of vanished suns, the peacefulness of dusk still floods my soul. O the peacefulness of beams of light on the plain !

Soon after the meal we ran to the pond; it became iridescent as it reflected the clouds.

At L*** M***, you remember, we would go at nightfall as far as the menhirs. Belated harvesters sang to each other as they made their way homeward on burdened carts; then their songs faded away in the distance. Crickets chirped in fields of wheat.

For a long time we would watch the darkness spread across the violet sea and rise like a tide from the depths of valleys, gradually blotting out all shapes. One by one on distant slopes lighthouses began to glow, and one by one in the distant sky the stars grew brighter. As we made our way homeward, Venus twinkled, caressing our eyes with her friendly light . . . .

And the night was descending on our ravished souls.[20]

In the morning you attended to your housekeeping chores. I watched as you passed through the long corridors in your white apron; I waited for you on the stairway, at the kitchen doors; I enjoyed helping you and seeing you at work; together we went up to the huge linen-room—and sometimes while you put away the linen I followed you about, reading a selection previously begun.

Then I called you Martha, for you were *preoccupied with many things.*

But in the evening it was again Mary, for after you were freed from the cares of the day, you again become contemplative.

. . . You had been assigned to Lucie's room.[21] It seemed that the dear departed one had not completely vacated it. When you moved in, the things that had once been hers seemed to recognize her and to come to life again. I saw everything as it had once been : the table, the books, the large curtains that darkened the bed, the chair where I came to read, the vase with the flowers that I had picked for you . . . . In the midst of all that you seemed to be reliving a former life, a life that had already been lived. Particles of *her* memory surrounded you,

[20] The choice of Brittany as the setting may have resulted from Gide's admiration for Flaubert. The interplay of setting, race, and religion may reflect the thinking of Hippolyte Taine, whose works were of especial interest to him during the period of the composition of the *Notebooks*. An interesting parallel between the two Andrés can be established on the basis of Taine's three great factors (Race, Environment and Epoch): Walter's Breton mother was a Catholic, his Saxon father a Protestant; Gide's Norman mother came from a Catholic family, and his Protestant father traced his ancestry to Languedoc; both were the product of two bloodstreams, two regions and two faiths; the anguish of both was caused by the interplay of Taine's three factors.

[21] Lucie was an older sister whom André Walter had lost in 1885. (Gide's note.)

making you more pensive. In the evening I saw *her* profile in the blurred silhouette of your bowed head, and your voice reminded me of her whenever you spoke. And soon both of your images became blurred in my memory.[22]

They had faith in us and we in each other; we had adjoining rooms.

Do you remember the lovely evening when I returned to you after we had said good night to them?

August, 1887

'Sleep claims all that surrounds us and through the window opened to the stars on this summer night come the sporadic cries of nocturnal birds or the rustling of moist leaves driven by puffs of wind, as soft as a lover's whispered words.

'We are alone in your room, overcome by tenderness and passion. In the caress of the air, in the smell of hay, of lime-trees, of roses; in the mystery of the hour, in the calm of the night, something ineffable causes tears to flow and the soul to escape from the body and to coalesce in an embrace.

'One against the other, so close that we are embraced by the same shudder, we magniloquently extol the May night, then when nothing more remains to be said, we remain silent for a long time and watch the same star, believing that the night is infinite and letting the tears on our cheeks flow together and fuse our souls in an immaterial embrace.'[23]

Rising earlier than the others, we would hasten to the woods on sunny days. The forest shimmered with cool dew and the

[22] The influence of the older sister illustrates Gide's technique of abstracting and reinterpreting in terms of his own psychology. It has been suggested that the older sister is identified with Gide's mother—the symbol of purity and the one who keeps Emmanuèle (Madeleine) and André physically apart even as she makes possible their mystical union.

[23] This passage recalls the Tristan legend as well as earlier and later writings that stress gratification through denial: the Orphic cult and Platonism, the troubadours and chivalric tradition, Dante, German Romanticism.

grass sparkled in the sun's rays. In the valley deepened and etherealized by the haze, everything was wondrous. Everything breathed new life and extolled the new day : our souls were lost in reverence.

Stimulated by our intoxication with these things, we longed to see the sunrise—a vain desire since the days were long. I came at daybreak and tapped softly on your door; you were only dozing; you arose and dressed hastily. But the house was still asleep, all the doors were closed, and we were unable to leave.

Then in your room with the window open to the cool dawn, and our bodies slightly chilled even though pressed closely together, we watched the last stars fade away and the tinged haze appear. Then when its crimson turned to brightness under the sun's first rays, morning songs echoed through our giddy, empty heads and we went back to sleep, intoxicated by our joy.

Tuesday

Multiply emotions. Not just one life in one isolated body; make your soul the host of several bodies. Feel it vibrate to the emotions of others as well as to your own and it will forget its own griefs when it ceases to think only of itself. The outer life is not violent enough; more poignant tremors result from inner surges of rapture. Let it feed on admiration; then it will be haughtier and its vibrations stronger. Not realities but chimeras, for the poet's imagination brings out more clearly the ideal truth hidden behind the appearance of things.[24]

Let the soul never fall back into inactivity; it must be nurtured anew on surges of rapture.

---

[24] The notion of the role of the poet in bringing out the truth hidden behind the appearance of things, though probably suggested by Schopenhauer, was nurtured by the Symbolists. Gide defended the doctrine of the Symbolists in his second work, *Narcissus* (1892).

The White Notebook

Plan of Conduct[25]

Freedom: reason denies it. Even if it did not exist, still we would have to believe in it.

We are shaped by definite influences: we must therefore discern them.

Let will be dominant everywhere: we should do as we please. We should choose our influences.

Let everything serve to instruct me.

3rd June, 1887

'I wanted to speak of many things, but everything besieges me. I wanted to devote some attention to my *Symbolism* which is now taking shape, but then came the memory of Notre-Dame and the white-robed children's choir seen by lamplight behind the railings of the main altar. The children were all singing and their voices were clear, creating the impression of an angelic choir; a minor cadence, relentlessly repeated and always unexpected, rose to the top of the vault. I also wanted to speak . . . but my thoughts drifted aimlessly, borne along by the melody of a quartet recently heard. I write because poetry overflows my soul and vainly seeks expression through words. Emotions transcend thoughts . . . and yield pure harmony.

'. . . Then words, disconnected words, tremulous sentences, something resembling music.

'It is midnight and I am sleepy but unable to sleep, for I am consumed by love. Everything around me sleeps; I am alone and I weep. The air is warm and it is raining outside—a spring rain that makes all nature fruitful. And the air played on the cello and remembered during the night assuages my delirium, lulls, soothes, consoles. Thoughts of grief, of madness, of love, of ecstasy are lost in restful sleep . . . .

'. . . Submit, my soul; weep and pray for a long while as sweet

[25] Pages rediscovered (note by André W.). (Gide's note.)

night brings intoxication. Weep and submit, my soul. Pray.'

1887

'. . . Or flesh in disguise. Rotten flesh! It appears everywhere in disguise.

'Consider the source of poetry . . . writhings of desire and nerves vibrating to the fascination of colours because of a small quantity of fluid dispersed throughout the body! Oh, what prose, what sordid prose at the bottom of it all!

'But such is responsible for the flower, the supreme poetry of the plant. Here diapered petals unfold themselves beneath erect stamens, like a sumptuous bed of unconscious delights. O poet's unconsciousness! blindness! vain belief in an inspiring Muse! Puberty excites the poet, making him wander about on starry nights under the illusion that he is extolling the ideal . . . until verses elude him. Then the stream of poetry that overwhelms him is converted into orgies in the arms of a courtesan.

'The derivative is indeed sublime! Indeed, it makes man think of himself as God! Beautiful, moonlight nights that evoke pure poetry (Musset) . . . but dogs also bay at the moonbeams!

'What is pure and what sullies cannot be known, for the connection between the two essences is so subtle and their causes so intermingled that a vibration in one is manifested in the other. An abundance of blood makes a generous heart. If Swift had known love, he might have written psalms . . . . And you tell me, friend, that I should not worry about my body but should let it pasture in the fields that it covets. But the flesh corrupts the soul, once it has been corrupted! New wine cannot be put into rotting vessels! The flesh lays claim to the soul unless the soul wins control at the outset. The soul must be the master and not the slave.[26]

[26] The allusion to the courtesan probably has no parallel in the life of the author. We learn from his journals, however, that he began at an early age to practise the solitary vice that caused him to be expelled from school, to incur his mother's disapproval, and subsequently perhaps to associate sin with sex.

' Then I am romantic because my blood pulses within me . . . .
Even so, the illusion of the ideal is good and I wish to preserve
it.'

Poubazlanec, September, 1887

'Your advice is striking, O Ar***. And so is your theory!
"Free the soul by giving the body what it asks!" you say. And
you would hold me in even higher esteem if I did . . . . But
friend, the body would have to ask for what is possible; if I
gave it what it asks, you would be the first to raise a hue and
cry; besides, could I satisfy it?[27]

'Your complacency is also striking! "The struggle naught
availeth," you said to yourself. "The soul must not exhaust itself
in unworthy conflicts." Yielding beforehand, you spared yourself
the effort. But you must know that gangrene of the flesh infects
the soul. No desire of mine fails to reverberate throughout my
soul.

'And you set yourself as an example. Certainly, I admire you.
Your outlook is broad and you take life as life will probably
take me eventually. But what I have not told you, what you
must never learn lest your serenity be disturbed, is the complete
shattering of my dreams when you, obviously disillusioned, told
me all this. Oh, I had placed you on a higher plane! And tears
on my wounded pride whose futility I suspected for the first
time! Disgust bordering on nausea on looking at life, the life
that must be lived! I prefer my dream. My dream![28]

[27] It is possible that this is the first allusion in any of Gide's writings to
his sexual aberrance.

[28] From earliest childhood the author evidenced a vivid imagination and a
preference for dreams in contrast to reality. His answer to a question put
to him in his old age might be cited to support theories he first formulated
on the basis of Schopenhauer's *The World as Will and Idea*. When asked
whether Madeleine was the model for Alissa, he replied, 'She *became*
Alissa.'

35

'You smiled as you said these things and I smiled as I listened, but I no longer understood your words. One thought alone made tears flood my heart: "He returned to the girl and was not recognized by her."

'Not recognized! Lord, is it possible? My heart ached throughout the night. Why this sadness? Such things must be. Why should she have recognized him? She had seen so many afterwards, and features inexorably fade from memory.

'But he had given you everything! Did you know? Had he dared tell you? How depressing is all this, how depressing! Fie! If this is the life that must be lived . . . .

'I prefer my dream, Lord! I prefer my dream.'

July 1887

'I detest their advances, their whispered or subtly intoned words, their ghoulish or siren voices—I detest everything about them.

'And when I walk down the street, I leave the sidewalks and quickly take to the pavement. From a distance I see them turning, pacing back and forth . . . and their gestures, their supposed designs for ever intrigue me. I would like to find out . . . .

'It was two years ago and it was for the first time. As a matter of fact it was the only time, for now I am careful and walk at a distance from them. One was singing a sad refrain; a little mockingly but tenderly, and with such a thin, weak voice . . . . As I passed near her she turned around and made a sign, without stopping her singing.

'It was the first time, one of the first nights of spring. The air was warm and the melody nerve-racking . . . . Tears filled my eyes. I could not help turning and running away. She laughed shrilly and another one who was loitering nearby called out: "There is nothing for you to be afraid of, pretty boy." The emotion was so violent that I thought I would faint; blood rushed to my face; I blushed from shame, from shame for them; I felt that I had been sullied by the mere fact that I had heard their words. My temple throbbed, my eyes were dimmed by a flood of tears. I ran away.

'But I shall remember the singing shadow beneath the blooming chestnuts, the flickering gaslight and the warm, distracting spring night; then the burst of laughter, as sharp as a broken object; and the tears that I shed. Yes, I shall always remember. The episode was unusually poetic.

'I am writing these things this evening because the season is the same, because the air is just as warm and because everything helps me to remember. I had played the scherzo by Chopin that I still remember and, afterwards, I ran through the countryside, intoxicated by sonorities, harmonies. The sky had no moon but was bright with stars; although there were no clouds, rain began to fall, warm rain almost like dew.

'And the air was filled with the perfume of moist summer dust.'[29]

Friday

I kept thinking about it until it became an obsession. Last night I dreamed that I was following a path lined by shadows and that on both sides of me writhed naked couples. I could not see their bodies but sensed their embraces. I was overcome by dizziness and, to avoid stumbling, was walking in the middle of the road, alone and erect, with my eyes raised to keep from seeing anything and my hands raised above my head. In the sky shone a few stars. I heard their love-making in the shadows.

I read in the Book of Revelation words containing mysterious promises:

Thou hast a few names which have not defiled their gar-

[29] Noteworthy here is the characteristic link between sex and sin, attraction and repulsion with respect to the same object, and the practice of employing external surroundings as memory aids.

ments; and they shall walk with me in white; for they are worthy.

He that overcometh, the same shall be clothed in white raiment.

To him that overcometh will I give of the hidden manna— a white stone on which no man knoweth saving he that receiveth it.

Then I meditated and made virtuous resolutions.[30]

My dreams were splendid. I wrote:

March 1886

'I would like at twenty-one, the age when passion bursts forth, to subdue it through frenzied, intoxicating toil. I would like, while others pursue vain pleasures, merry-making and debauchery, to taste the sequestered delights of the monastic life. Alone, absolutely alone, or perhaps surrounded by a few white-robed Carthusians, by a few ascetics; sequestered in some rustic Carthusian monastery in the open countryside, in a sublime and stern setting. I would like to have a bare cell and to lie upon the floor with a horsehair pillow under my head; nearby, a huge but plain praying stool; in the alcove, the Bible always open; overhead, a lamp always lighted. I would like during periods of sleeplessness to experience violent raptures in the terrifying darkness that envelops me as I become totally engrossed in the study of a verse. No noise except perhaps the occasional heavy rumblings of mountains, the dismal voices of glaciers or the midnight psalms chanted on a single note by the Carthusians who keep watch.

'I would like to live fully with only time to pursue me: to eat when hungry, to sleep whenever I chose once my task had been

[30] His *Journals* reveal that Gide's virtuous resolutions were made repeatedly only to be broken whenever his demons overpowered him. The *Notebooks* represent his first attempt to escape through his art from the clutches of his demons.

completed. I would wear the white mantle, scapulary and sandals. In my cell I would have a huge oak table and on it, wide open, a few books; a big lectern for working while standing up; rows of books above the bed. I would read the Bible, the Vedas, Dante, Spinoza, Rabelais, the Stoics; I would learn Greek, Hebrew, Italian; and my mind would take pride in its vitality. There would be orgies of learning, and the mind would emerge stupefied, broken, as did Jacob after his struggle with the Angel—and, like him, the victor. And when exasperated flesh rebelled and erupted in a rash of desires, pain caused by the lash of discipline would soon quell the body! Or a frantic race through the mountain, past cliffs and as far as the snow, until panting flesh cried out for relief, exhausted, vanquished ... or a plunge into deep snow—and an extraordinary shiver resulting from the icy contact.'[31]

As a very young child I was ignorant of some things to which I had been exposed.

'Later on,' I thought, 'I will not have mistresses. All my loves will tend towards harmony.'

I dreamed of nights of love in the presence of the organ. The melody was an almost palpable fiction, like a nebulous Beatrice, *fior gittando sopra e d'interno*, like a chosen Lady, immaterially pure, with the deep-blue folds of her trailing sapphire-studded gown shimmering in the pale light and slowly assuming musical patterns. I hoped that she would receive all my tenderness. I was a child and thought only of the soul; I was already living in a dream world; my soul was freeing itself from my body; and my dream of better things was exquisite. Later I separated them so completely that I am no longer the master; each goes its own way, the soul dreaming of ever more chaste caresses and the body carelessly adrift.

[31] Parts of the *Notebooks* were written while the author was in seclusion near the Grande Chartreuse. He viewed the monastery, considered visiting it as a tourist, decided against the visit

Wisdom would dictate that they be kept in check, that their paths be made to converge, and that the soul not seek distant loves in which the body cannot share.

'They do not complain; they make accusations. They do not explain; they condemn. What they will never understand is the struggle to BELIEVE, waged against impossible odds so long as the slightest degree of reason protests. They think that the will to believe is enough! And the most astounding part is that they think they can believe through reason. What especially outrages me is mock religion; bigotry and pretended mysticism sometimes make me doubt that there is a true religion. Bigots are not aware of the harm that their example can do to those who truly seek after the true God; they are not aware that in their complacency they are often themselves an object of scandal . . . ."[32]

Midnight, 30th December, 1887

'Shall I write? . . . What?

'I am happy.

'I am afraid of forgetting.

'I would like for the memory of my happiness to endure beyond time.

'If only it were possible in the boredom of the tomb to relive life incessantly and to feel gently, as in a dream at night, bitterness and joy—but from such a distance as to cause no more suffering than the memory of griefs.

'I am afraid of forgetting.

'On these pages I wish to preserve—as one preserves dried flowers to recall dissipated perfumes—I wish to preserve the memories of my fleeting youth in order that I may recall it later.

---

[32] Gide seems here to anticipate his own paradoxical development, which prevented the consummation of his marriage even while permitting him to father an illegitimate daughter.

'Today I spoke with her. I told her my radiant dreams and my high hopes. Today I understood that she loved me still. I am happy! . . . What shall I write?

'I write because I am afraid of forgetting.

'And now all of that is only in my memory . . . .

'But perhaps the memory of old things still subsists beyond the tomb.'

It was in a wretched room. Poor people were weeping over their dead child (7th February, 1887). I had come without saying anything, for I did not want her to find out until later. I brought them some money; I wished that I could comfort them. I forced myself to speak to them but was embarrassed by my exalted ideas; my sadness on seeing them was certainly sincere, but I experienced it in such a different way; I do not know how to humble myself. I dared not speak to them about heaven since my own belief was too weak; I was uncertain and ill at ease even though my heart was overflowing.

Now I saw the door opening. Emmanuèle entered.

'Is it you, Emmanuèle?'

She passed in front of me with no show of emotion, as if she did not see me. She stood next to the bed where the child lay. She looked at its pale face and I saw her eyes fill with tears. I drew near her and tried to grasp her hand with mine.

'No,' she said, pushing me away.

Then kneeling, she prayed aloud. Retreating to the shadows, I heard her sad prayer and felt humble. Then she departed, and I went with her. While walking along, I kept hoping that she would say something about our meeting, but she was too overcome by emotion to comment on it. Her words were meant to explain her sudden departure, or perhaps to break the embarrassing silence.

'Let us leave them,' she said. 'It is good for them to grieve. Let us not console them now. Our words would not be sincere. Their hope will be renewed by their tears. We must come back, for a kindness cannot be left undone once the first step has been taken; it is an obligation that must be fully discharged.'

But no sooner had we returned than she put her forehead against my cheek.

'My brother,' she whispered.

Her emotion was now too much for her. As she raised her eyes I saw that they were filled with tears. Compassion sapped my strength, but her confession of utter helplessness compelled me to be strong.[33]

I asked her—diffidently, since both of us were overly modest about such things—I asked her to return to the place with me. There she was sweet, patient, sincere—and paid no attention to me; I was attentive only to her and did my utmost to elicit a compensatory smile . . . . But the end soon came.

'Watch out!' she once told me, 'Your concern is for me, not them.'

Once again I was separated from her.

Providence : their life in its entirety is based on a hypothesis; if they were shown their mistake, they would no longer be able to justify their existence. But who would show them? They will never know whether or not they were mistaken in their belief. If there is nothing, they will never know the difference. Meanwhile, they believe; they are happy or find consolation in their hope. The doubting soul is torn asunder.[34]

'Philosophize? What arrogance! Philosophize with what? With reason? Who guarantees us the soundness of our reason? What is the source of the authority which we accord it? Our only

---

[33] Frequently in Gide's writings we find an allusion to his concern for Madeleine, dating back presumably to his discovery of her mother's infidelity and his intense longing at that time to protect her against the harshness of a counterfeit world.

[34] These same notions form the substructure of *The Immoralist* (1902).

assurance would be in thinking that it is a gift of a providential God—but reason denies God.

'If we argue that reason came about by a slow transformation, by a gradual adaptation to phenomena, we may well discuss the phenomena—but beyond that?

'And even if we grant that it comes from God, there is still nothing to guarantee us of its infallibility.

'We can only hazard opinions. An affirmation is open to criticism, for it is arbitrary and destructive.

'Narrow minds which think that theirs is the only truth! Truth is multiple, infinite, as diverse as there are minds to think—and no truths are challenged except by the mind of man.'

Everyone is right. Things BECOME true as soon as someone believes in them. Reality is within us; our mind creates its Truths. And the best truth will not be the one sanctioned by reason. 'Men are guided by emotions and not by ideas.'[35] 'The tree is known by its fruit,' and a doctrine by what it suggests.

'The best doctrine is the one which through its message of love will persuade man to worship joyfully; which will comfort in times of distress by offering a vision of happiness promised to those who mourn; which will call grief an ordeal and enable the soul to hope in spite of everything. The best doctrine is the one which offers the greatest consolation. *Lord! To whom would we go? Thou hast the words of eternal life!*

'Reason will ridicule but, in spite of all philosophical objections, the heart will always need to believe.'[36]

'ΣΥΜΠΑΘΕΙΝ—to suffer together, to vibrate together. Imagination is all powerful, even in matters of the heart. Charity

---

[35] Ribot.

[36] The conflicts between faith and reason, appearance and reality, carnal passion and ideal love are familiar antinomies that motivate much of Gide's art.

depends on our ability to imagine the griefs of others and make
them our own. Thus is the life of the soul multiplied. And thus
does compassion assuage grief.

'A heart vibrating to the emotions of all men, throughout
time and space, and doing so voluntarily though spontaneously :
that is what we need.'

We used to read aloud on autumn evenings when they had
assembled between the hearth and the lamp. Thus we read
Hoffmann and Turgenev.

Everyone listened, but the modulations in my voice were for
you alone. I read to you over their heads.

We studied German together, though we already knew the
language. The lessons were a pretext for leaning over the same
book and being excited by the discovery of subtleties of meaning
as we translated passages.

That is how we became acquainted with *Die Braut von
Messian, Die Heimkehr,* and *Die Nordsee.*

German has whispered alliterations which make it a better
medium than French for expressing vague yearnings.

One evening it was raining and those who had gathered there
had been talking for a long time.

'André,' said V***, 'will you read a little?'

I began the *Expiation*, which she did not know. It is indeed a
soothing work. Reading the words with subtle inflections, I made
the violent emotions that were flooding my soul flow into yours.
ΣΥΜΠΑΘΕΙΝ: to experience together violent emotions.[37]

I did not see you. You were sitting in the shadow, but I felt
your look when I read :

And their souls sang in the brass bugle.

The sun was setting. Evening shadows were invading the

[37] The notion that in Madeleine he had found a kindred soul (an Echo for
his Narcissus) persisted for years in Gide's imagination despite indications
to the contrary on her part.

room. No longer able to see clearly enough to read, I closed the book and recited:

Not one retreated. Sleep, heroic dead! . . .

When the lamp was brought in for us, it seemed to awaken us from a dream . . . .

'Listen,' I said to you. 'Pay close attention to what I am saying.'

I wanted to go over a difficult problem concerning German metaphysics that had bothered me for a long time. I saw that the attempt to follow my reasoning was causing wrinkles to mar your brow, but the obstacles that I had already cleared goaded me onward, and I continued to speak. I would have liked for our minds to travel together along every byway; I suffered when learning without you; I needed to feel your presence; I thrilled to your emotions more than to my own. But these heights were too lofty; your spirit fluttered helplessly and grew tired.

I suffered much over such things. When you were not there and overpowering emotion forced me to speak, my mother soon tired of my expositions, for she lacked your benevolent patience. When she became listless, I fell silent and my rebuffed soul shivered in its solitude.

I was then a child. I did not understand that the mind is nothing and passes away while the soul still remains after death.

The mind changes, grows feeble, passes away; the soul remains.

'What is the SOUL?' they will ask.

The SOUL is our WILL TO LOVE.

We still said 'brother' and 'sister', but with a smile. Our hearts were no longer deluded. Yet you wanted to be deluded. You were afraid that we would go too far, and you hoped that you could allay your incipient fears by using a familiar word as a decoy. You thought perhaps that the word would evoke

45

the thing and that if we always called each other brother and sister, our relationship would be fraternal. But in spite of our intentions, alien inflections marked our words; they became more intimate, more endearing, more mystical when whispered to each other. When you said 'my brother' and I answered 'little sister', our hearts quivered at the involuntary tenderness of our voices.[38]

Long autumn days . . . sitting by the fireside while rain fell outside . . . engrossed in reading for hours at a time . . . and you sometimes came to lean over my shoulder and read.

I was reading *The Golden Ass* when you came, as was your custom, to read over my shoulder.

'This is not for you, little sister,' I said as I pushed you away from me.

'Then why are you reading it?'

You smiled somewhat waggishly—and I closed the book.

Playing games during our childhood, seeing landscapes, conversing at length, reading together when we knew nothing and could discover everything together . . . .

All these things mean nothing to others but gradually shaped us and made us so nearly identical . . . .

A stranger, Emmanuèle? . . .

Would a stranger remember the beloved dead?

Oh that he had never known them! Oh that he had never seen their smiles! When you chose to speak of them, he would not understand. Then you would fall silent, aware of your loneliness.

(incomplete)

I no longer know either where or when : It was in a dream.

[38] Gide's fraternal relation with his cousin Madeleine probably began at an early age. He was present at her father's funeral in 1890, just as she had been present at the funeral of his father ten years earlier.

One night I was weeping for both of us—and your dear shadow came close to me. I felt your hand on my brow and saw your sweet smile.

But I was still weeping.

'Well, do you want to, André . . .?' you asked without moving your lips. Your smile illuminated my soul.

In my soul I have kept the music of your words, and on my brow the memory of your sweet caress.

28th May

The last three days I have reread your letters. I have kept them all, but they give a poor impression of you. If they were all I had to remember you by, I would think you waggish, rather fickle, always evasive and elusive. Your mind forces your soul to remain aloof.[39]

From time to time, however, it would suddenly cry out to me, and it was then so plaintive—like a prisoner.

'Do not withhold your affection, my brother,' you said. 'I prefer it above all else.'

And later on, after a separation, you said: 'I cannot accept the idea of life without you.'

And there was still more. There were fleeting moments of tenderness, quickly squelched by the mind; then in the next letter, ironically you made fun of yourself and of me for having believed you.

The reason was that far from me, your mind was again dominating your soul.

Yes, sometimes your soul managed to break free, and when it spoke, its ardour astounded even me. At times I questioned your tenderness since you refused to acknowledge it to yourself; I thought that I loved you much more.

[39] Frequently and for many years Madeleine's actions apparently belied Gide's hopes.

The last night before we were to part for a long time, I told you these things and wept—as much from emotion as from the wish to be assured by you—for I was comforted by only the most tenuous hope, and when I was uncertain your absence made me fear the worst. But you finally tired of the silence.

'Oh, André,' you exclaimed tearfully, 'never will you know how much I loved you!'

Your mind is stubborn, despotic. It would have you be domineering. You again resorted to mockery. Oh the smirk on your lips! I had to obey immediately or you would evade me. Silence until I gave in. You knew that I would always come back to you. That was what made you strong; I was not sure of you; I gave up quickly.

Then came sweet reconciliation. We managed to be together more often, and our souls were all the more loving when we were apart because we had restrained them.

Your mind! I will find fault with it because it irritates me. It is your mind that I know best, and yet it is not similar in any respect to my own. You are afraid to admire without passing judgment. You would like to keep your reason unimpaired; whatever is immoderate terrifies you—as much as it attracts me. I resent your not having trembled in the face of Luther's grandeur; then I sensed your femininity, and I suffered. You understand things too well and do not love them enough.

But our souls—they are so alike that they cannot know each other! . . .[40]

I wrote to Pierre:

But let them believe. What right have you to deprive them of the joys of believing? What will you give them in exchange?

[40] Madeleine, though frightened and insecure because of her childhood experiences, was older than Gide and had enough common sense to refrain from marrying him until after his mother's death. It is doubtful that the two ever fully understood each other.

They are absolutely right even if they are mistaken. To believe in possession is as comforting as to possess . . . and are not all possessions chimerical? They are duped by a mirage of eternity and uplifted by their hope. If there is nothing after life, who will return to tell them? Nor will they be aware of not existing after death; they will never know that they have not lived on eternally. But nothing must stand in the way of their belief here and now—it is the basis for their happiness.

I remember having shown her those lines.

'O André!' she exclaimed. 'If things were the way you say they are, faith would be an illusion. Only truth is worthy of belief, even though it might offer no hope. I prefer to suffer through not believing than to believe in a lie.'

Ah! Rebel!

Your serene and lofty ideas are too much for me. I am tormented by the stability of your faith; I wish it had tottered. Oh, that your soul had cried out in the void! Mine would have been less forlorn with yours for its companion, for it would have known compassion. You might now be less haughty. But you did not flinch, and now you look down on me.

Then one day we were reading Spinoza—oh, how these memories tire me!—and admiring his divine plan.

'Does this not bother you, Emmanuèle—this unorthodox book?' I asked.

'Oh, all doubts are in the mind,' you said. 'A book could not create them.'

Sweet little soul! Who could know it?

Our minds were intimately acquainted and no longer withheld their secrets. We knew each other's thoughts before speaking and we knew how they would be phrased. I made a game of it. When we were talking I would anticipate the word that was to come from your lips and take it away from you before they parted. But familiarity with the mind did not extend to the soul . . . . One soul pursued the other but was always deluded and led astray by the succession of thoughts that flowed in parallel fashion through our minds. The soul was enchanted by an illusory similitude, one that involved not the soul but a frivolous mind.

It was like the lover in the legend of Ondine. Pursuing her one evening, he imagined that he saw her changing image in the will-o'-the-wisp hovering over a pond. Seduced by the captivating illusion, he dashed after it only to be disillusioned. He wept when the phantom disintegrated between his fingers.

(Our souls were obscured by our thoughts. When one of them darted forth, it would skid along smooth surfaces. The slope formed by our thoughts was so inviting and the succession of our thoughts so effortless that our souls were tempted to go wherever our thoughts coincided.)

We liked to lose ourselves in distant memories. By virtue of associations that transcended time and space and unsuspected relationships, one word was enough to evoke a host of dreams. The word was never bare but it had one and the same legend for both of us; it evoked from the past many emotions, many passages that we had read—both when we had said things and when we had read them. It was never the word itself but the recall of the past. That is why we derived so much pleasure from quoting poets—not because we experienced something through them but because they reminded us of so many things!

Then one word often signified a whole sentence known only to us—it was only a bare word to others. One word was the beginning of a verse or of a thought, another marked the end. For instance, when we were walking around the house one evening, I began:

Listen! my dear . . .

and you understood:

The White Notebook

Listen to the night gently descending.[41]

Then it became a task, an obsession. We had always to watch for companion thoughts and to bring them to light even though we recognized them for what they were beforehand . . . . We no longer thought but watched each other think, and with the same result. But we were tormented by the need to test the similitude and would voice our thoughts even though we could have remained silent and communicated without words.

We anticipated sentences, snatching them from each other's lips before they were uttered—and sometimes as we both waited for a thought from the other, the same thought would come to both of us.

On summer evenings it was with Chopin, Baudelaire . . . .

Leisurely dreams the moon tonight . . .
How would I love you, O night, without stars . . . .

But our tired lips left the verse incomplete and we let our eyes give more precise expression to our feelings of tenderness tinged with desire.

Some of those around us were upset by our close relationship, which we never tried to conceal. They tried to separate us, to erect barriers between us; but it was already too late, for we communicated by means of signs unnoticed by others. Instead, they quickened our interest in the mystery of sign languages, and we created our own solitude in their midst. By shackling them, they revealed to us our desires.

'Phenomena are signs that make up a language—the language of the desires that lie behind phenomena. Only desires matter, and they must be understood.

[41] Pierre Louis praised Gide for his choice of quotations, particularly this one from Baudelaire (and gave rise to the suspicion that he considered the quotations superior to the text).

51

'To understand is nothing, but to be understood—that is the problem and the source of anguish. The soul throbs and would have the other know—but cannot and feels isolated. Then come gestures, words, awkward explanations and material symbols for imponderable outbursts of feeling—and the soul despairs.

'Nor is that anything. The worst suffering is that of two souls unable to approach each other. *Thou hast built a wall around me to prevent my going out* (Jeremiah).

'They hug the wall that keeps their courses parallel, and they collide and bruise each other.'

'Neither words nor gestures give shape to thought—they proceed from the frivolous mind. But the inflection of an excited voice, the lines on the face, especially the look—these are the eloquence of the soul. Through them the soul finds expression. They must be studied, dominated, made into docile interpreters.

'I study them in front of a looking glass. They would have laughed if they had seen me looking into my own eyes and, by night, becoming almost hypnotized by the changes undergone by dark pupils as I searched for the outward manifestation of emotions through sparkling or sorrowful looks, for the alignment or narrowing of the eyebrows and the wrinkles on the brow that should accompany words of passion, of elation, of sorrow . . . .

'Comedian? Perhaps . . . . But I play myself, and the roles best played are those best understood.'[42]

'Then it becomes painful never to lose sight of myself while searching anxiously for the word, the gesture, especially the look and the inflection of the voice which will best reveal the secret emotions of my soul.

'Often preoccupation over appearing to be excited supplants

---

[a] Paul Claudel once rebuked Gide for his fascination with mirrors. Gide completed his first book and simultaneously practised the art of self-scrutiny by setting down his thoughts as he stood before a secretary equipped with a mirror.

the genuine emotion. Many times I have been with you, Emmanuèle, and felt the true, spontaneous emotion vanish under the attempt to force it to the surface.

'Suffering consists in being unable to reveal oneself and, when one happens to succeed in doing so, in having nothing more to say.'

To understand each other is nothing. What matters is a mating of our souls.

'I need to caress someone. My repressed caresses have not been restricted to one person but lavished on everyone. My caress is an embrace; I tend instinctively to embrace others.'

The sad part, and the part that has caused me to suffer acutely, is that the soul can reveal its tenderness only through caresses which are signs of unchaste desires. The soul is mistaken, deluded . . . . And then in me the gesture awakened the thought . . . .

I must remain frigid in order that there be no mistake, even on the part of my soul . . . for sometimes . . . . I must simply clasp and release her hand, bid her good night without the kiss of peace. My heart may quiver—but imperceptibly and not violently.

'Loving, adoring, impassioned caresses—I am obsessed by the act of caressing. I would like an all-absorbing, all-encompassing caress, or complete oblivion of self, which constitutes ineffable ecstasy. That is why I suffer so much in the presence of the beauty of statues, for then my being does not blend with theirs but contrasts with it.

> . . . *Quoniam nihil inde abradere possunt,*
> *Nec penetrare et abire in corpus corpore toto.*

'A little flesh is still infused by virtue of the transparency of the marble. The desire to possess torments me and I suffer piteously, both physically and spiritually, through awareness of the impossibility of possession. I am corrupted, not intoxicated, by the sight of the *Thorn Puller, Apollo*, the mutilated torso of *Diana Reposing*.

Nec satiare queunt spectando corpora coram.

'And I suffer still when I think that they will never feel my caresses.

> *Superfluous, implacable splendour,*
> *O beauty, what pain you cause me!*
>
> *Impossible union of souls through bodies*
> *. . . tormented by an embrace.*

'Here is the strange part, and the part that has caused me to suffer so much. The soul blends in with everything else, and it becomes impossible to determine whether it harbours desire or whether the flesh is disguised as reverence. *So insistently is the soul pushed towards the mysterious bed . . . .*

> *A caress comes to an end, is ephemeral,*
> *My soul stirs at the sound of a kiss . . . .*

'*Et non erat qui cognosceret me . . . .* Nor the others, for souls cannot know each other. The courses followed by those who are most nearly alike are still PARALLEL.

'So you see that I do not desire you. Your body disturbs me and carnal possession frightens me. We do not love each other according to the dictates of rational love. You could never belong to me, for the things that we long for are never possessed.'[43]

---

[43] This section seems to recapitulate Gide's adolescence and to anticipate his predicament after he had realized the full consequences of the complete separation of (carnal) pleasure and (ideal) love. His reaction to statues is recorded in his *Journals*, and his sensuousness and sensitivity to physical contact endured a lifetime and caused him alternately to tend towards renunciation and affirmation of the desire 'to remain carnal unto death.'

The White Notebook

A letter from Pierre and some books. He writes of Paris, of the struggle and of some early triumphs . . . . Farewell to philosophical calm; this gust of feverish air intoxicates me and rouses dormant visions of glory. My ambitions were slumbering in solitude, but now they have been awakened. Everything militates against my secluded life : a flurry of excitement, of preparations back there. I shall arrive too late for everything.[44]

The letter is really good for me. My pride is cut to the quick but I am not defeated. The lash that brings the blood gives me the energy to run even faster. Oh, how strong I feel !

I shall arrive suddenly, without warning, and blow a loud trumpet blast—or perhaps remain unknown but hear my work acclaimed (for I shall withhold my name).[45]

I must work frantically, *dishonestly*. I shall leave here only after the work is finished. And to avoid further disturbances, I am having my mail sent to an imaginary place.

His writing is perfect—callously, impeccably, inexorably so. This discourages me, for to me my language was still fluid and boundless. I wanted to give it rhythmic contours—but emotion always made the sentence explode, and I set down only the debris.

[44] Gide was convinced that he had something to say to his generation, that his problem of formulating an austere ideal to free him from temptations of the flesh and protect him from anguish was a familiar problem, and that his time was limited. Though he had long nurtured the project, he was not able to begin writing systematically until the spring of 1890, when he, aged twenty, broke away from his mother for the first time and secluded himself at Menthon, near Grenoble. He felt that before the age of twenty-one he had to finish the work—and he did.

[45] Pierre Louis achieved fame (as Pierre Louÿs) before Gide and knew him during the period of the writing of the *Notebooks* but not during the year assigned to it in *The White Notebook*.

The Notebooks of André Walter

The books are by Verlaine, and I did not know him!

This evening, even though the hour was late, I trimmed and stacked the paper that Pierre sent with the books. The sight of white paper intoxicates me. The black signs which I may use to cover them, which will reveal my thoughts and which when reread later will recall today's emotions.

I could not sleep because my simmering thoughts were so uncontrollable. I felt the pressure of latent creative forces. Inspiration became something tangible, and the vision of my work was as dazzling as if the work had already been completed. What splendours of aureoles, what flashes of dawn! Then my burning brow, my grandeur stunned me—disorganized thoughts—the feeling of stumbling, a fall—something on the verge of breaking . . . . Oh, loss of sanity! Suddenly, piously, gripped by indescribable terror, I made a supreme effort to protect my mind and my vision against sudden destruction.

'Forgive me, Lord,' I prayed. 'I am but a child, a small child lost on a treacherous byway. O Lord, keep me safe and sane!'[46]

Let style and mood blend. And since this is not plastic art, let music exert its influence. Why not even a strophe?

Put your hand in mine, and let our fingers join,
Put your chin on my shoulder, and let our hearts beat as
one,
Let your brow come to rest and let your eyes merge with
mine.
But let us stop short of a kiss, for fear that love will intervene.

Let us not speak but listen to the singing of your soul
And to the reply of mine through fingers joined;

[46] In *The Black Notebook* (the Manichean twin of *The White Notebook*) we learn that he does lose his mind but not before entrusting his notebooks to a friend for possible publication.

The White Notebook

Hearts in close communion, looks that reciprocate . . .
Silence—let us not speak.

> *Your soul sings in your dark eyes.*
> *Come closer to me, my friend,*
> *You are always too far away.*
>
> *Closer, ah! come closer still—*
> *How upsetting are your glances!*
> *They seem to smile and your soul to cry.*
>
> *How far behind your pupils is your soul.*
>
> *Into the damp darkness of your eyes*
> *Plunges my desire-drenched soul*
> *But your soul keeps retreating*
> *Behind the darkness in your eyes.*

'Dearly beloved, ah! turn away, ah! turn away from me
Your eyes, for they disturb me.'

(Alternate: Schumann)

Do not look at me. Speak to me instead—I am listening.

> *Oh! speak and I shall see you in my dream*
> *Not unlike the inflection of your sweet voice.*
> *Words are unimportant—speak incoherently,*
> *Speak slowly, think of the harmony*
> *That your soul will reveal to me.*

I would like to be lulled to sleep by your words.

Sometimes I think that pursuit of the elusive soul is a deception and that the soul is but a more subtle manifestation of the

57

mind; reason then advises me to rejoice. Priceless subtleties then ensue:

The effort that my soul makes to reach yours must be instinctive, spontaneous. It must be unconscious and the soul must be lost . . . in self-contemplation.

Still other subtleties.

They will not indulge in calling and in contemplating each other. If they escape from the body and leap towards each other in a mutual outburst of desire, they collide or their paths cross, but there is no place for them to come to rest.

The result is that they meet in mutual admiration and inter-mingle on the thing admired. They will thus be oblivious to themselves and will not be troubled by enticing looks, and will not exhaust themselves in the attempt to call each other.

For example, I have at times experienced their fusion when we were reading and admiring each other—when both of us prayed for each other in the mourning room with Lucie, when we watched the same star on a flowery May night and let our tears run together as our cheeks touched and we surrendered our souls to each other.

Still other subtleties—traps set by the bantering mind.

'Our communion is still not perfect.

'I sense the confusion in our souls; I do not sense their fusion.

'In order for mine to blend with yours, I must lose the notion of its resistant life, its consciousness of itself. Then the soul becomes passive.

'Thus nirvana is experienced only as the taste of nothingness in non-life itself. It is negation.

'Our communion will never be perfect; or, if perfect, it will never be experienced as such.'

But harmony—music! Music carries the undulation of one soul all the way to the other soul.

Bodies hindered me; they hid the souls. *The flesh is useless.* An embrace should be immaterial.

Possession. An alternative for Allain—and for me. If only I could be convinced . . . .[47]

At night when the body surrenders to sleep, the soul escapes. It flies hurriedly towards distant loves and possesses them immaterially. The body dreams.

Morning comes and the body stirs, awakens, rises. Again it takes possession of the little soul, which is again imprisoned. Distant memories are cause for regret—dear loves recalled merely as dreams . . . for normally you are accompanied by the body, little soul! People do not imagine caresses in the absence of bodies. Ah! If they knew! But they are all blind!

And each evening my soul flies to your side, to the side of the one loved by my soul. Like a weightless bird my soul alights on your lips, and with a slight tremor your lips begin to smile.

With a passionate (*sehnsuchtsvoll*) shout my soul summons yours. Like two merging flames our two souls fuse and plunge more deeply into space filled with harmonies produced by the beating of their wings.

They have taken their flight through space. It is night and the moon is beautiful. From vast sleeping forests rise masses of fog. Together we fly towards sweeter heavens, towards warmer breezes whose caresses our souls desired.

Through pines where the wind sings—in the forest chilled by sparkling dewdrops that fall on us as tears from sagging branches

---

[47] The enigmatic conclusion may express doubt—conscious or unconscious—on the part of the author. In this section and others we find parallels to Manicheism, based on the doctrine of the two contending principles of good (spirit) and evil (the body).

—over wheat that extends beyond the range of sight on the empty horizon and inclines at our passage, like a billowing sea traversed by gusts—to moist slopes where the petals of dormant flowers, finally refreshed, perfume the stars with their ecstatic dreams.

Through the night's silence our souls pursue their swift untroubled flight.

Death when it comes will not separate our souls.
Beyond the tomb they will take flight and again join.
For separation of bodies does not make soul solitary.
The world can only separate bodies.
Nothing can stand in the way of the loving soul, for love has conquered all.
Love is stronger than death.

'Reason' they say, and to me this is sheer arrogance. What has their Reason done?

It is always contrasted with the soul; when the heart acts, reason interferes.

It is repulsed by devotion. The sublime is always ridiculous. Daring, poetry—everything that makes life worth living is foolish. Reason would protect us; it is utilitarian, but it makes life intolerable to the soul.

It is despised by true lovers, for one who loves no longer lives for himself. His life is but a means of loving. If he finds one which is better and which will make for closer union, he will neglect—perhaps reject, forget—his own life in favour of it.

I have never had any happiness which reason sanctions.

August 1888

'It was already late and the others, tired, sat down to wait for us.

'The other hillside, ascended with great difficulty, sloped

gently downward. The sun bathed the plain in golden, peaceful rays. At a bend in the stream was a castle with a slate roof; around it were the lower roofs of white farmhouses; under a thick fog was the pink heath and, protruding above it, a crest of grey rocks.

'The foliage of two chestnuts blended above our heads. On the slopes of the meadow, women were stacking hay; amorous sounds filled the air; and hovering over and enveloping everything was a radiant serenity, a penetrating tenderness that seemed to emanate from things and rise with the odour of the hay when night came. Our souls were refreshed by the setting.

' *"Lord,"* I exclaimed, *"it is fitting that we remain here! Would you like to? Let us pitch our tent!"*

'Then you smiled, but your smile was so sad that I sensed in it your desolate soul. My own shuddered for an instant. You understood too much and, quickly turning away in your fright, you sadly broke the spell.

' "Come," you said. "They are waiting for us. We must leave all this . . . ." '

Emmanuèle and I begged her to sing. We were alone.

V*** sat down at the piano and began to play and sing Schumann's *The Sorceress.* Her voice was but a puff of air, a fragile vase of emotion—it was pure emotion, with nothing to contain it as it escaped ethereally, revealing her soul. It seemed that the soul itself was singing and replacing her voice.

When she came to the high-pitched notes in the bewitching line *'Es ist schon spät; es ist schon kalt,'* she trembled and quivered like a broken object.

Your emotion was too much for you; tears poured from your eyes; then, ashamed of your confusion and worried because your heart also quivered involuntarily, you darted away. I followed you to your room.

'Oh, leave me!' you said. 'Please leave me!'

I went away. I wandered until evening through the fields, my mind undulating with the flood of exaltations produced by remembered harmonies.

Let my soul sense its vitality through the effort to win in its arduous struggle. Then will come dreams of the impossible, of chastity, of faith. Then, endowed with new strength, it will be brave enough to overpower your soul in spite of your belligerent mind.

Your mind! I once resented your mind, your poor mind which was frightened by your troubled soul and which did its utmost to calm your outbursts of feeling. What struggles! And always to resist yourself! You wanted your will to prevail and you set it against invading tenderness.

'I shall never allow myself to be dominated by anything!' you thought.

I misunderstood all that. I only understood that your mind deprived me of your soul and that your soul desired me.

I sometimes hear your soul cry out softly, but your dominating mind subdues it. One day I shall force it to cry out and prevent your mind from stifling its pleas.

One day I shall force your poor soul to speak . . . .

Music, music—in anguished harmonies your astonished soul will recognize its counterpart and release the tears that it has long restrained. But when I start to play, you become alarmed and flee.

One summer night—a hot stormy night following a splendid day—all was still without. There was no breeze. My soul was expectant.

You came out on the terrace while the others remained inside. When I saw that you could not flee, I opened the window wide and sat down at the piano. The sounds came to you in waves.

I began to play Chopin's first *Scherzo*—brutally, noisily, almost as a prelude at first, for I did not wish to startle your soul. When I came to the *più lento*, I muted the melody and it cried, morbidly sweet. As pearls drop from a fountain, the high notes fell, obstinately the same but severally eloquent, while the harmony changed.

I went back to the *agitato* but with all the passion in my heart, making the anguished dissonances quiver. I stopped abruptly before you could break the spell. And I approached you and found you trembling; there were no tears and your eyes were radiant.

'André, why were you playing that?' you asked, and your voice was so different that I was frightened and dared not answer.

We remained silent.

'Look into the darkness,' you finally said, as if alarmed. 'Is it not supernatural?'

Lightning flickered noiselessly on the horizon. The air was perfumed with pollen from lime-trees, with the scent of flowering acacias. I tried to take your hand; it was feverous but you rebuffed me.

We remained silent.

'Oh, André,' you again interposed, but in a whisper and with your head lowered, 'you acted cowardly this evening.'

Raindrops were beginning to fall. We went back inside.

The storm broke during the night. You were suffering: feverish and almost delirious.

The next day you stayed in bed and refused to see me.

'My affliction is not serious,' you said.[48]

Thursday

'My thoughts kept me awake almost all night long. I could

---

[48] Soon after his arrival at Menthon, where he was writing the *Notebooks*, Gide installed a piano. Though he was an accomplished pianist, he is said to have played his best when no one was in the room and when he suspected that someone outside was listening.

not sleep. "Oh, André, you acted cowardly this evening." Suddenly I felt you next to me, so frail, so fragile—as if penitent.'

'It was wrong for me to do what I did : to upset you, to wish to disturb your soul . . . . And could I satisfy it after altering it?'

'*You acted cowardly!*

'Her contempt! Do not hold me in contempt! . . . What now?'

5th October

'All day long I experienced infinite sadness amid grey surroundings.

'I collected one by one my sullied hopes, and I cried over each of them.

'All my strength had left me; I no longer dared even desire you from afar.'

'I ceased to pursue your soul.

'I shall wait. I shall be there. I shall still be the same. If you have the slightest desire for me, I shall rush to your side—but not until you call me. I shall wait.'

Sunday

'Today I lived close to her but our eyes did not seek each other. I did not draw near you. I was lost in thought almost all day long.

'Waiting.

'We shall travel PARALLEL. That used to drive me to despair.'

'I have again started to read my Bible. I must once again ascend the slope which I descended unsuspectingly.

'Oh, how difficult it is!'

I skip over pages—the transition will be too abrupt, but I am tired of recounting everything.

I would like new things—and I see some that are so radiant . . . .

I was sad then . . . . How distant is this 'then !' Outside spring is in the air—and I would like to sing :

For the day is approaching, the dawn draws near.

18th October

'Self-esteem, contentment in the soul! The splendour of virtue, which I at first sought for you, gradually dazzles and attracts me.

'There are loftier emotions, nobler yearnings, more sublime raptures.

'The soul evolves.'

22nd October

'For me alone! For me alone!

'They will not understand—what does it matter to me?

'My heart is flooded. I must sing.

'A little harmony rather than words—no sentences—Oh for words that they might understand!

'*My heart teems with incantations.* My soul floats on a moving tide of modulations and broken arpeggios which rise like a troubled flight of furtive wings and incessantly fall without being resolved.

'Passion flows rhythmically, metrically, quietly . . . passion subsides; the soul meditates.'

'ALLAIN.

'In order not to taint her purity, I shall abstain from caressing her—in order not to disturb her soul—and even from the most chaste caresses, from clasping her hand . . . for fear that she may later desire all the more that which I could never give her. And I shall not look into her eyes for fear that she may wish me to come closer and cause me in spite of everything to go so far as to kiss her.

'In this way our souls will remain fearful even though one calls out to the other . . . .'[49]

25th October

The soul meditates:

No virtue without effort. My chastity is not virtuous. I love to love because it is sweet for me to love and because I would be loved as much as I love . . . but there is no effort.

Nor does effort count if motivated by the desire for the esteem of another—for her esteem. The effort must be made without hope for reward.

I am searching for the source of virtue.

Virtue would consist in doing good without her knowing about it . . . yes, without my laying claim later to a larger measure of her esteem . . . .

Without her knowing . . . and wilfully—is this possible? First, before acting, I would have to promise not to say anything to her—about the act, nor to anyone who would repeat my words to her—to bury the act in my heart. It is at this point that the idea of God is necessary. I would have to appear to myself to be offering it to her like a secret sacrifice whose smoke would rise to her without being seen by men—to promise myself to hide it for ever! . . .

But this thought tantalizes me: 'What would be the use then —since she would not know about it?'

Mercenary! The reward for good must be found in the good itself; we must not expect it to come from men.

Or take the reward of meriting her esteem—of feeling that when I approach her, I am worthy (a little more worthy at

---

[49] Highly significant in that it anticipates Gide's conduct towards his wife after their marriage, this passage suggests both her role as the mother-sister image and the presentiment of his inability to consummate a physical union with Madeleine, 'the only woman he ever loved.'

least). Oh, without my saying a word, she would read it in my eyes, would look past my eyes into my soul . . . .

'Never mind,' she would say. 'I know without being told.'

Here again, her esteem would be involved. To be sure, I would have advanced, but not far enough. What else?

I would have to be vilified by her until my rebellious pride crumbles; to accept the unjust accusation without trying to defend myself in order that she might think me worse than I am. That would be struggling, heart-break, triumph!

But suppose that as a result she loved me less?

Well, now! that is the acid test. Virtue consists in feeling that I am above her esteem, that I am more worthy than she thinks. That she would love me less matters not, for I would love her all the more; this would be my reward. I would not be deluded, for I would know that my actions were motivated by the need for self-esteem, by pride; still, I would accept the inevitable, loyally, simply, without pretending to wage gratuitous moral battles with myself.

Yes, that is how things stand. Virtue consists in suffering the loss of her esteem. I must lose her esteem—but how? A lie through which I discredit myself? No, the act itself must be thoroughly pure. The best way is for me to let things drift along, simply, ordinarily; this will cause me to suffer the most, for I am afraid of being encouraged by the test itself, by some slight theatrical element which I might introduce into it.

Then, simply, ordinarily, I shall let myself be discredited by things, by all those things that surround me, by the infinite number of petty, accidental accusations that will cause my aggravated pride to bristle; but I shall restrain it and in the evening, very calm and very lonely, I shall pray and shall slowly kill my mutilated ego.

And I shall love you still more, bless you still more, my sister, because I shall whisper to myself (but not to you) that it is to you that I must become better.

I must deserve you by leaving you—(oh! artless).

'The more abundantly I love you, the less I am loved.'
(II Cor. 12 : 15).[50]

'For me alone! For me alone!

'They will not understand . . . but what does it matter?

'I shall always recognize you, dear tears of love, under the mystery (to others) of these sobs, these pleas, these laments . . . .

'Tears? Why tears?'

'I am happy, however . . . she loves me . . . but my soul trembles when night falls.

'In the street they laughed in passing. I did not know who was singing, but the voice was too loud. Then evening came and stillness reigned. The water reflected the pink sky, except under dark bridges.

'And I did not know—I walked like a fool. My head was filled with songs.

'Then evening came and stillness reigned . . . shadows lengthened—and pale night appeared in the pale sky . . . great encompassing night.

'Tears? Why tears. Tears of love, of ecstasy!

'I weep because the night is beautiful and hope floods my soul.'

Midnight, Antibes, 5th November

'It is night. I cannot sleep. What are you doing, Emmanuèle? I know that you lie awake. On the balcony the light from your room silhouettes the flowers embroidered on your curtains. What are you doing? It is late. The others are asleep.

'And what was wrong with you this evening? You seemed pensive—pensive over what, my sister? Oh, if only I dared read

---

[50] Alissa, André Walter's feminine counterpart in *Strait Is the Gate*, also practises humility and self-denial in pursuit of Christian glory; as in the case of all other Gidean heroines, she succeeds. She dies and Jerome finally possesses her, recalling again the Tristan legend and the tradition of fulfilment through denial.

your soul! . . . Emmanuèle, could it be true? . . . But I am afraid to find out—I wait for you still.'

Oh! I beseech you, daughters of Jerusalem,
Do not awaken, do not awaken my love—
Until she wills it.

I sat down at the piano. I had not dared to play for you again since the other evening . . . fearing the worst, doubting. I played at random Schumann's *Novelettes.* You were on the balcony. It was still warm in spite of advancing night. I played at random—and then—you came to listen to me. I had not seen you approach but suddenly the delicate rustling of your dress made me aware of your presence. I trembled so from surprise and confusion that I could no longer play.

'Look!' I said, 'You upset me so much when you come up like this . . . I am trembling.'

'Why, André? Why?' you asked with a smile.

You did not go away. You remained nearby—and you watched me. I felt your look without seeing it.

Turn your eyes away from me, for they disturb me.

You remained so pensive. Pensive over what, Emmanuèle?

What are you doing now that it is so late? The hour for sleep has come.

Then—a little later on—we were all sitting around the lamp. You had risen to look for a book and then, before you sat down again, you came near me and I felt your delicate hand gently caress my forehead.

I looked at you; bending over me, tenderly, you were smiling, but sadly, pensively . . . . Pensive over what, Emmanuèle?

What are you doing now, so late at night?

Perhaps your soul is also waiting and you are praying.

6th November

'For the first time I saw your look in a dream.

'You were smiling, but mockingly. I put my hand over my eyes to avoid seeing your look, but I could still see it through my hand.'

'You told me at the kiss of dawn : "I prayed for both of us last night, André."

' "Do you think that I did not know, little sister?" I replied.

'Then you looked disturbed; you wanted to speak but fell silent. What did you wish to say?'

26th November

They are watching us, I know. Especially my mother. She dares not believe; she does not know—and is afraid to find out. She is especially disconcerted by the fact that for the past several days, for reasons incomprehensible to her, I have avoided you. But yesterday when you came up to the piano, I could not help noticing her uneasiness.

Then I had a dream last night, a strange, sweet dream. We were sitting by the lamp in the evening—talking, reading as on other evenings—but I sensed on all sides their mute spying on our movements, as one senses things intuitively in dreams.

Fearfully I observed my actions. Frightened by the notion that you might approach me, I had sat down far away from you.

You, absent-minded, apparently unaware of their looks, came up to me : I was unable to run away, and your hand sought mine as it tried in vain to escape and slowly, tenderly, caressed it.

Around us their faces became animated, their heads nodded, their smiles appeared.

'Aha!' they said, 'we knew it all along, all along!'

Their derisive laughter seemed forced. You kept your eyes lowered and continued obstinately to caress my hand, which I tried in vain to withhold.

And that was so strangely sweet that I awoke, as from a nightmare.[51]

Here end the written pages.

My mother was sick. We stood by her bedside and comforted her. I cooled her brow and you gave her water. Both of us were engrossed in a common prayer; all else was forgotten. Our souls, void of everything except pity, void of desire other than that of serving, united in the face of approaching death, not in profane joy, not even startled by the ecstatic embrace long anticipated and finally realized—and almost without seeing each other because of the dazzling light of virtue which we contemplated and towards which our souls aspired.

All else was forgotten, so lofty were our thoughts.

In the evening you put your hand in mine to pray; then you forgot and removed it as you watched my dear moribund mother fall into peaceful sleep. We remained beside her for a long time.

Both of us kept watch that night in the room where the dying woman slept. Though near, we did not see each other. That was the supreme moment; our souls evolved. Without speaking, as if in a trance, we thought—what thoughts!

Virtue, which first I had sought for you, now dazzled me and exerted on me its pull . . . .

The boundaries of reality were blotted out; I was living a dream.

---

[51] This entry strongly suggests that Gide blamed his mother for interfering with his plan to marry Madeleine and extricated himself from the painful situation by idealizing his love for both. Blinded by his own emotions, he was unable to appreciate the soundness of his mother's advice to her niece or the perceptiveness of the latter in rejecting his proposal.

The next day my mother spoke to me. I have already repeated her words . . . but the sacrifice had already been made
in my heart . . . .

Then my mother set their engagement. I know that I saw both
of them, Emmanuèle and T***, at the foot of the bed, their
hands clasped, and that my mother was giving them her benedic-
tion. But all the rest is forgotten—my overwhelming grief seemed
unreal and I thought that I was dreaming—there was no longer
even a trace of bitterness in my grief.

And what remains now is joy . . . .

28th June

Some evening I shall recall the past and repeat my words of
mourning . . . . Today, however, the sky is too bright, too many
birds are singing. I am inebriated by spring and my mind is
filled with new lyrics in which our name delicately rhymes and
alliterates with the names of flowers. It is a sweet melody : an
air played on a flute—almost like the warbling of birds—and
the sound of wings beneath leaves in visible shadows—O flutes,
soaring oboes ! . . .

Love transcends mourning and death.

And the allelujas of victory will drown out the song of the
willows.

Bless you, beloved mother ! Above your bed of suffering our
souls found each other again.

You could separate only our bodies, enabling all three of us
to find comfort in the serenity of studied virtue; but through
a higher, inscrutable will stern virtue, which seemed at first to
separate us, became glorious and consummated the chaste desire
in our souls.

It is through obedience that I have found her again—in spite
of ourselves and because it had to be that way.

Then I departed.

As soon as the period of mourning had ended, they celebrated their marriage . . . their marriage . . .?

And I departed.

I departed, and took refuge in this solitude, for I no longer knew anyone . . . *after the flesh*, as the apostle says.

And I am going to write my book.

How changed, my soul! how changed!

You once wept but now you smile.

Do not study yourself—explain nothing—let sentiment rule; and then—forge ahead . . . . All things have been renewed . . . .

I said to my soul:

'Why are you smiling? You are hopeless in your solitude. It is as if your erstwhile friend no longer existed. You will have to cease your adulterous dreams.

'Weep. They are gone, all your loved ones, and have left you alone. Weep. Your loves have ended. The time for love is over . . . .'

'Do you believe this?' my soul replied, still smiling and repeating to itself:

Love transcends mourning and death. Acute sorrows have been blotted out and the willows are silent.

Sing, my soul, to new dawns.

All hopes have blossomed anew.

THE BLACK NOTEBOOK

Pro remedio animae meae

BEYOND TIME and space I address to you these pensive words in order that their distant echo will reach you. Did you know, Emmanuèle, did you know that we were in love? Your love has taken all my soul, which now sends to you its fragrance. Now I return to you what you have given me: your music and poetry. Listen, my soul sings. It sings of things past, of things remote in time, so that you may know at last how enduring was our love. And lest it too pass away, I confide to the breath of the wind these senseless pages. They will consume the chaste desires of our souls and consummate our eternal betrothal.

1st July, 1889

Strange, finally to undertake the work contemplated for two years.

Friday 5th

I have begun a new notebook which I want to reserve for the book. Yesterday I set down its general design and outlined its contents.[1]

---

[1] Here begin the first notes recorded by André Walter for the composition of his novel *Allain*. We thought it necessary to publish them in order to avoid destroying the integrity of the manuscript, but we have separated them from the text since they are only distantly related to the rest of the diary—P. C. (Gide's note.)

[Translator's note: Gide uses the initials P. C. to identify the friend to whom André Walter entrusted his notebooks and his novel. Here, as elsewhere, I have tried to reproduce Gide's uneven style, even when the result is disconcerting.]

Monday 8th

Yesterday I went for a walk. I was tired of work. My soul flagged under the weight of my body.

Se col suo grave corpo non s'accascia . . .

I walked in the darkness in order that nothing should distract me. Along the road. The sky was dark, and the wind breathed a dewy coolness.

I reflected for the first time on the fact that you still lived, but I was no longer made joyful by the thought; and that someone else now possessed you, but I was not jealous. Jealous of what?

And since our thoughts, at the same time, had always been the same, I wondered whether our remembrance of thoughts would perhaps be the same also—were you remembering, Emmanuèle?

Two actors: the Angel and the Beast, adversaries—soul and flesh.

There is no such thing as materialism, not any more than idealism (literally speaking). There is only a struggle between the two. Realism demands the conflict of the two essences: that is what I must show.

Not a realistic truth, inexorably contingent, but rather a theoretical truth, which is absolute (at least from the viewpoint of mankind).

Ideal, yes! According to Taine's definition: the appearance of the Idea in its pristine purity. It must be made to stand out from the work. It is a demonstration.

Therefore, simple lines, schematic arrangement. Reduce everything to the ESSENTIAL. Tight, sharply outlined plot. Characters reduced to one—And how intimate is the drama;

77

Surely, in this short time your thought has not strayed from the familiar path that guided it towards me! During unguarded moments, old reveries may reappear. My memory clings to so many fortuitous images, frivolous in the case of others, evocative for you alone—evocative of the past.

Everything speaks to you of us, incessantly, and reminds me of you: a scent, a flower that I had plucked for you, a word, a passage read, a gesture, a caress. Oh! you remember, Emmanuèle! You remember and you love me. A thing is not quite dead that is not yet forgotten: you cannot forget our love. You love me still, Emmanuèle—and in spite of yourself, for present duty goes counter to your memories and reason whose protection you desire seeks to quell the uproar of your bruised affection.

If I knew what you are doing, I could imagine what you are thinking.

---

no part of it appears on the surface—not a fact, not an image, except perhaps one that is symbolic. Phenomenal life is absent, there are only noumena; therefore, nothing is colourful and the staging is neutral; the setting can be anywhere at any time—beyond time and space.

Only one character, just any character, moreover, or rather his brain, and this but the common terrain where the drama unfolds, the enclosed arena where adversaries do battle. The adversaries are not even two rival passions, but only two entities—the SOUL and the FLESH—and their conflict which issues from a single passion, from a single desire; to be angelic; it issues from a necessary deduction, as a conclusion from premises set forth.

The premises:

Body and soul: Man himself; the soul tends to ascend—the body weighs heavily.

The Black Notebook

Tuesday evening

The shadows have increased and lengthened. The plain is transplendent with the last rays of the sun. Now the sun has set—evening songs as in times past. Times past . . . our souls were transplendent in the mutual reflections of our ecstasy, and I heard in you the echo of my silent adorations.

Then night came. I began : *Listen, my beloved* . . . . And you understood : *Listen to the night gently descending*— The refrain of verses learned by heart and recalled from the past along with other memories.

> *Pâle Vesper, lumière dorée*
> *De la belle Vénus Cythérée*
> *. . . O claire image de la nuict brune!*

That is the sum and substance of it.
Spinoza's prescription for Ethics : *transpose it in the Novel!*
Geometrical lines. A novel is a theorem.
I would like for the form to be so lyrical and so moving that poetry would spill from it, in spite of its rigid lines.
Oh those straight lines! Props! But I would like to have, encircling them, convolvuli and wild vines.
Lyrical form, the strophe, but without metre or rhyme—only cadenced or scanned—or rather, musical.
And not so much the harmony of words as the music of thoughts—for they, too, have their mysterious alliterations.
Let the rhythm of sentences not be external and false—the mere succession of sonorous words—but let it undulate with the flow of cadenced thought, through a subtle correlation.
Diction! At first I thought that I would have to submit to it,

79

It was night, the very night in spring when we were both in your room—I remember. We were looking at the same star, both of us—and our eyes, lost in the act of contemplation, met once again in that distant mirage—the immaterial embrace of fused souls.

And other nights—do you remember, sweet sister? It was three years ago, at S***, after we had been laughing, all day long, and sharing in the gaiety of the others. Our laughs were hearty, but laughter stirs some tenderness deep in the soul. That evening, having returned to our rooms, we gave in to an indefinable resurgence of sadness and we wept and prayed well into the night, frightened by the joy that had been ours, thinking of Lucie and all the dear ones who had left us, and as for-

---

but I soon rebelled against its demands: then I had an urge to dominate it, but it refused to submit: and since neither of us would give in, and I cared little for it, I finally abandoned diction and deliberately fashioned a language of my own. Should I write in French? No, I would like to write in the language of music.

Soul. The power of the word is lost through repetition. It would be better to say angel—*despite its etymology. Who knows its etymology?*

In the angel, the ever growing desire to ascend. He must have a goal and move towards it: it is towards you, Emmanuèle, ideally superior. (And there, the impossible novel in its entirety.)

As for the flesh, there is no need of it. The force of gravity alone, quod pulvis est, *hampers the angel's ascent. But there must be a progression.*

lorn as the Book of Ecclesiastes upon which we had long meditated, our minds exalted by too lofty thoughts and deluded by
the vanity of desires, and our hearts broken by an infinite love
discharged as tears and prayers.

I did not know that you were praying, and you did not know
that I was weeping, but each of us through some strange
intuitive act of the soul, sensed vaguely what was happening.
And the next morning, without saying anything to each other,
look probing look, transparent, but for ourselves alone, to the
depth of our souls, we both saw that during the long vigil we
had been weeping and praying.

No, the body is not an indispensable interpreter. There are
more subtle communions, embraces of which it knows nothing,
and the gentlest caresses are exchanged beyond space—when it
is in repose.

This evening I looked at the star—and you too, perhaps,
Emmanuèle! Recalling evenings in the past, perhaps you too
dream of new nights.

Why should I pity myself, and what have I lost?

Friday 11th

Finished the first part of *World*[2] and, for the second book,
reread and took notes on Kant's *Logic* and the *Treatise on the
Syllogism.*

Logic ought not to be studied for itself. It is a captivating
game from which the mind draws strength. That is why Stuart
Mill excelled in his *System*, but I do not have it with me.

*That which knows all and is known by no one is the Subject.
It is therefore the support of the world . . . .*

What exaltations. Let me shout this sentence with all my
might, and lose myself in this sublime thought.

---

[2] Schopenhauer's *The World as Will and Idea.*

At the piano

Night—very faintly, a sweet, drowsy melody evokes a dream. imagine *her* presence—forget things—dream.

For a long time I was lost in uneasy drowsiness. The air was warm for the first time, and the scent of acacia reached me through the open window.

12th July

The first thing is to write at random—but this I no longer know how to do, for the vision of my work pursues me. To it I subordinate all else. Gone are the happy days when I could write with no concern other than that of writing and when my head teemed with turbulent thoughts.

Now everything has its place, the aim is well defined, and everything supports that aim . . . . Farewell to refrains thrown to the wind; so much the worse if they are lost.

But I must wait and see. Spring is scarcely here and already my heart thrills to the expectancy of unknown ecstasies . . . . Perhaps new songs will spill forth.

On sort sans autre but que de sortir.
Verlaine

Uneasiness pervaded my body, anxiety forced me to go out—for the sake of going out. I paced between my desk and the window, yearning for fields that stretch to the horizon, for enticing coves, for pleasant meadows.

What will become of me, Lord, if spring excites me so? I thought that I had been freed . . . . Surely chastity is beautiful and its splendour tempting—oh, fie on all the rest! But if every fibre in me is aflame and if my dream consumes me . . .?

But is what you require of me not possible, Lord? *No temptation has come upon you that was not human, and God who is*

82

faithful will also send you the strength to overcome every temptation.
The fields are in bloom.
Platacumque nitet diffuso lumine coelum . . . .
I must write something—in alexandrines—five stanzas, feminine rhyme repeated in the last verse of only eight syllables :

'Enough of love, my Lord! My soul is now possessed!'

I long to express dispassionately—in plain song—the hopelessness of feeling myself dominated by the blind impulse of fresh sap, and the desire—still without declamation—to take refuge in chaste thought, in the noble life of abstract speculation.

I have reviewed my Greek grammar and my algebra—against these importunate fires, mathematics is a capital remedy. I must immerse myself completely in study so that physical stimuli will not distract me.

Sei ruhig Pudel! renne nicht hin und wieder!

Tuesday

Numbers are fascinating. In them we glimpse and come into contact with the absolute. The will is stimulated and presses onward in pursuit of the problem; it knows that afterwards comes rest, calm assuagement in the realm of the immutable. But just as it is about to seize the absolute, it is frightened by its silence and, always indefatigable, turns away only to undertake new pursuits. The contemplation of the results is in itself dazzling : therein is the source of the fascination of numbers and of the intense curiosity stimulated rather than assuaged by discovery.

There is in a well-balanced equation a purely aesthetic eurhythmy which I find intrinsically seductive.[3]

[3] Under the signature of André Walter, Gide had published his first writings, 'Reflections from Elsewhere—Minor Studies in Rhythm', in the literary review *Wallonie.*

I have again taken up *Ethics*. I am copying the fourth book, ignoring the scholia so that I can grasp the general plan and understand the sequence of the proposition.

18th July

Spinoza—the serenity of your genius overwhelms me. Girded by your marvellous architecture, you saw the world through your work and were lost in endless contemplation of your projected thought.

And so we all live in a dream of reality. An atmosphere created by me envelops my soul and unconsciously colours my vision of reality. And, since it is impenetrable it imprisons me in solitude. And, since it is variegated, each vision of reality is individual. A man never sees anything but *his* world, and he is the only one to see it; it is a phantasmagoria, a mirage, and the prism responsible for the variegated light is within us.

Of these particular visions none can be called absolutely true; intransigence is foolish arrogance. But even if none of them are false, some visions are preferable, and not in themselves but by virtue of the emotions that they suggest: *the tree is known by its fruits.*

Spinoza's divine tranquillity is accessible only to the souls of the élite. What I admire in Spinoza is not so much reason itself but rather power, number, especially will, and then the rhythm of his system. I admire his divine tranquillity as I admire the *Iliad*, and without troubling myself over the question of its truth.

But I myself have had to have more than soul. I have had to have less elaborate but more vibrant things—things which appeal to the heart, make the soul quiver, agitate the mind. Then action, struggle, something foolish—imagination killing doubt, mind subduing flesh—something musical and productive of profuse poetry.

84

The Black Notebook

When I finish Schopenhauer I shall take up *The Origin of Species*. I have finished Berlioz's *Memoirs* and the second volume of Michelet's *History of France*.

Oh, how I would have liked that man!

The majestic ring of his lament: *My passion began the day my soul fell into this wretched body which I am wearing out by writing this* . . . .

How intoxicating! I live in a perpetual state of hyper-excitement. Outside everything is in bloom; summer bathes everything in light.

Saturday

Writing bores me, for what is there to write? Of all the emotions that demand expression, why choose one rather than another? Yet I must write, for my head is bursting under the pressure of accumulated emotions.

. . . What keeps me from writing anything, even premature notes, is the complexity of my emotions rather than their multiplicity. For if I had something definite to say, I would be able to formulate it precisely, but the slightest perceptions from without unleash within me infinitely complicated systems of vibrations which have their repercussions in the soul just as they have repercussions in the realm of physics, awakening dormant, latent ideas which find expression again and again in the context of new emotions . . . . Often I am seized by the desire to be surrounded by darkness and silence, by unbroken calm; beside me a lamp which would cast no shadows on the wall; time with neither hourglass nor clock—unlimited time to contemplate and to transcribe . . . .

Midnight

How gentle the breath of night; a caress
Wanders through the air; an amorous murmur

85

... The pale adolescents have vanished two by two in the shadows, and the air, along with the scent of the foliage, brings to me the echoes of their kisses and laughter, hints of their caresses.[4]

I will not go out. I will lock myself in my room. I will read and pray until sleep comes.

Eternal One! I look upon you as my refuge. May I never be deceived! But you, O Eternal One, how long must I wait? How long will you leave me alone? How long shall I struggle without feeling that beside me I have you whom I need in order to win? ... and later? ... how will the struggle end?

Sunday evening

In my body and soul is unbounded anxiety. I dream. Sporadic sounds of love-making around me stir my passions. I cry without knowing why. Odours intoxicate me as warm wine; I am drowsy; my soul is overcome by a desire for caresses. O my head on your shoulder, and your cool hand ....

> *O leave your hand where it lies, cool*
> *Upon the eyes whose lids are hot ....*

Remembrances! ...

I am alone:

I recall past days, bygone days, and I weep. The breath of memories lulls me, and thoughts—*overwhelm me like the deep.*

Oh! What pathos when one is at the threshold of happiness, when one can almost touch it—and when one passes it by.

Let the soul remain desirous always; let it hope. Life is nourished by anticipation; satiety makes it subside. Let prudent

---

[4] Gide's erotic adventures were purely imaginary prior to his first voyage to Africa in 1893.

maidens remain attentive. The sadness of regret is so sweet, especially when one has not known possession. It is evocative and stirs old memories. One recalls the past again and again, and desire remains even after sadness has vanished.

Summer evenings, festive nights, under chestnut-trees and in the shadow of ancient turpentine-trees, songs, sounds of revelry —the courtesans, the roving courtesans called out; from afar I heard their mirth . . . but we shunned facile delights.

Afterwards: the lamp, locked doors, study in solitude.

I also remember when I was returning one night from the home of Ar***, following our candid discussion and our laughter, and heard the hackneyed taunts which they shouted in the deserted street. 'Come on,' they said. 'Let's have some fun!' I left them and went alone to my room. Then, at the piano, I played until well into the night, overcome by dreamy languor; and for a long time, before falling asleep, my head propped on the bolster and numbed by fatigue and sadness, I wept—not from regret—but because I should have liked to know what they were saying.

Chastity!

. . . And for that, barren enjoyment wrung from suffering: *Surgit dulce aliquid* . . . .

I made the trip to Auvergne alone, on foot, and solely on account of my desire for intense mortification—to quell the pangs of restless puberty. Long walks in the sun, in the rain, in the dust of the roads; my spirit dull, my body exhausted: my flesh satisfied—and darkness, and the sudden onset of brutal, dreamless sleep.

And in the morning a new beginning and renewed pursuit of self-control through nagging fatigue.

When for the first time I set out to see the Chartreuse, the magnificent Chartreuse, I wandered for a long time nearby on the road from Saint Laurent to Saint Pierre. I kept looking at the cove where I knew it stood, invisible, and for the road that would lead me to it. But I did not approach the Chartreuse for fear that I might shatter a long-cherished dream. I turned back, delightfully sad and more pensive than ever.

Oh! What pathos when one can almost touch it—and when one passes it by.

Wandering Jew!

'Come, now!' you were saying. 'You must leave all that behind.'

At R*** the day before my departure, in the evening, I had climbed the hill. I was going to leave *all that* behind—and I looked into the valley of Thônes and at the unknown road which vanished in the distance that lay ahead of me and which I could have taken. Beyond lay new streams and mountains, beyond lay sparkling snow, forests and villages; and I repeated their names to myself in my bitterest sadness: Sallanches, Giettaz, Bluffy— the name of a cold Arctic fjord covered by blue mist . . . and then I departed without seeing anything else, leaving behind me my trail of cherished memories.

Oh! How sweet is the bitterness of disappointment over things one has never known!

Comme la nuit est calme; on croirait qu'elle prie.

I am sleepy. Lying at your feet—oh! I would like to put my head on your knees.

> . . . *Beloved hands that once were mine . . .*
> *O beloved hands, O cherished hands . . .*
> *Their cooling shadows on my eyes . . .*
> *Their silence enveloping my thoughts . . . .*

I would like to fall asleep . . . the heavy folds of your garments. To dream—to forget loneliness . . . .[5]
Emmanuèle.

---

[5] These lines suggest Verlaine's 'Les chères mains qui furent miennes'.

For Allain—parallelism of the passions.

The emotions are for ever interdependent and evolve in parallel fashion : pious love, love for Her, and often confusion of the two. But is there perhaps a constant correlation between the two—just as in the case of burning thoughts, intense concentration, and to an even greater extent, the call of unconquered flesh—and is it possible that everything depends on the latter since it in turn depends on the season and other unknown elements?

Philosophy of reason—it must in any event be studied even if knowingly ignored or forgotten later on under the stress of the emotion of the moment. To reason must be left that which pertains only to reason.

So, for Allain, the evolution of the passions must be so cleverly plotted that they stand out and illuminate each other, as if by a mutual reflection.

I must not write one page this way, one that way, but make a synthesis so that a part will reveal the whole, and so that an isolated part will suffice to reconstruct . . . etc. (Cuvier)

I would like at least to know whether flesh excites the spirit or whether the spirit corrupts—and finally, if a battle is to be waged, which of the two must be dealt with first.

Then, whatever I write for Allain, I must first tell to myself —my love for you will feed on pious prayers. Pious souls are loving souls.

Religion is love.

Intuitive knowledge is the only knowledge necessary. One must go beyond phenomena to contingent pluralities and contemplate ineffable truths. Reason becomes useless. It must be repudiated or it will come surreptitiously before our deluded eyes and stir up hazy arguments. The sciences are dangerous, for they exalt reason, which then speaks up and demands control.

Reading fires reason with pride. Why? When the spirit reads, the heart slumbers and its ardour cools underneath the dust of erudition.

So, I must not read any more, except for the Bible, which I must read at great length, and the classical sagas, which I must reread leisurely.

Thursday

Remembrance of past communions:

'I don't know. I don't know anything. You asked for me: I came.

'I don't know you. I don't know who you are or even whether you exist, but I have to love you to avoid having your divine heart grieve because of me just in case you are and you do desire me.'

And again:

'If I had known you, Lord, I would have loved you with all my soul. And I love you still even though I do not know you. I love you even if you are not, for you at least exist in my thoughts, and my thoughts project before me your image which I adore. If I had known you, Lord, I would indeed have loved you.'

To force oneself to believe when there is no recourse is sentimental sophistry. True faith does not require justification but simple belief.

The will must be annihilated, voluntarily destroyed. Virtue resides solely in struggle and only in the effort to subdue.[6] The

---

[6] In his preface to the definitive edition of the *Notebooks*, Gide stated that what he had once assumed to be the sincerest expression of himself was due solely to his puritanical upbringing, which taught him to struggle against his temptations. He added, 'I would not have been so thirsty if I had not at first refused to drink.'

first flames are not meritorious—this I understand clearly now. So long as reason has not spoken, belief requires no effort. Love is sufficient to inspire reverence.

O the first flames stirred by puberty! Ecstasy—I know that it is often sensual; and they too know it, and that is the reason for candles and incense and organs. For their voluptuous surrender to the arms of the divine one who was crucified is often shameful.

Solemn worship services and forbidding chapels have protected me against false prayers.

I have not worshipped graven images.

Sunday

Quia absurdum

Judge not.
And this applies to yourself as well as to others.
—And to things as well as to beings.
SPONTANEOUS LIFE
INTUITIVE KNOWLEDGE
FAITH

Monday 29th

> *De la musique avant toute chose . . .*
> *De la musique encore et toujours . . .*[7]

Music pervades my reverie, giving it direction and movement. Reason slumbers, my heart keeps vigil—and my soul? My soul quakes.

This is what I must do: benumb reason and sharpen sensitivity.

But for my will to remain attentive and my effort constant,

---

[7] Verlaine's 'Art poétique', written in 1874, was published ten years later in *Jadis et Naguère*.

I must practise. The scales are too beguiling—but rolling arpeggios, rough syncopation, broken chords and trills, these give metre, rhythm and direction to nascent thought. I must practise systematically instead of creating vague but pleasing melodies that enfeeble or aggravate my nerves.

Ah! Paolo and Francesca! Why was the eternal embrace of the shadow of their bodies sheer torture? Because desire had subsided. Possession during their lifetime, which had at first intoxicated their flesh, now filled their souls with nausea . . . .

I shall always desire you—and so the aimless flight of two souls implicitly joined is for me sheer happiness—the happiness of my dreams.

But your body holds my soul captive, and your overpowering mind . . . except perhaps in dreams, when the body relaxes and the mind falls asleep . . . .

Tuesday 30th

These rambling notes set down by fingers that have become very supple are in some ways ludicrous.

I have worked frantically: a vibrant atmosphere of restless harmonies surrounds me. Then constant, unrelenting effort: during the last three days I have memorized two new preludes and two new fugues from *The Well-Tempered Clavicord*. Reason slumbers, but how my mind teems with thoughts! And what voyages into the world of the imagination!

1st August

Schopenhauer.

I must lose the sense of its relation to things, so that the representation will stand out in all its purity, with no external knowledge to distract me from intuitive knowledge and *suddenly tear me away from my primary vision.*

If I could manage to contemplate illusion so attentively that my eyes were dazzled and would no longer pay the slightest heed to existing things around it, my illusion would seem real to me; and if I evoked an image from the past, I would forget that it was from the past and make it something wholly present to the extent of blotting out existing things. What I lack is the power of constant attentiveness. My attention too often flags, and the image that I have evoked immediately becomes once more a mirage.

Music must intervene.

Yesterday evening I played for a long time, until the silent hours when only vibrating chords broke the stillness of the air. Slowly, unconsciously I lapsed into an ecstatic trance and darkness became luminous to my visionary eye.

'Ah, still delay, chimera!'

Music is suggestive; it is the supreme enchanter; it sustains the flight of dreams.

And this is what I imagined: you came to listen to me, as you did one evening—and then you stayed there, pensive and speechless; behind me, by bending slightly, I felt your breath on my forehead. And you were saying, but not through words, for it was less than a thought: 'Why were you crying? Here I am. What is past is past, what is present will remain.'

The winged melody, in spite of the tears we shed, spread far and wide our new happiness. The breath of spring was coming through the open window. If I had turned around, I would have seen you . . . .

> *Night has claimed the dormant hill.*
> *Silence reigns; the voice of night is still.*
> *Birds sleep; all is at rest . . . . Night . . .*
> *Through sheltered nook and cove,*
> *Through silent open spaces*
> *Go departed souls of those in love*

Along paths that they had trod
While searching living lovers' faces.

When lovers die, they do not go straightway to heaven. For a long time still when mysterious night arrives, their souls wander through all the places they have loved.

When night falls departed souls spring out—blurred couples merged in an immaterial embrace or lonely, searching individuals—and move like a breeze through silent clearings.

They are delayed in their journey to heaven, held back by their past loves. Like aimless breezes they wander—along accustomed paths in the country—and without speaking they remember. Their embraces, when relived, are like a wedding of their new and former loves.

By night meadows have gentler slopes, wooded regions grow denser, and valleys are attired in silver spray.

O Nights! These beautiful nights are much more conducive to contemplation than the others.

More tender is the secret caress of the starlight, and in the soft darkness their love shines forth as a star.

The souls of the departed wander over the heath; others, near ponds, gather as in a dream sheafs of sleeping flowers or, along solitary pathways, strip the leaves from imaginary chrysanthemums.

Dear enamoured souls detained far from the promised land —they loved too deeply on the earth—they can no longer tear themselves apart.

. . . Where one is all love and the other all grace.

. . . I recall that she used to prop her head on her hand while reading. She would often bend over, her head almost on her shoulder. But I also recall her bending over me, protecting me. I would lift up my eyes and see her looking humbly at me.

I must picture her exactly as she was.

And what else? Lingering memories, meditation, prayer, sweet joys of a pious soul, and then even greater love for you . . . .
Oh! If only your soul were not in captivity! . . .
(*The following page is left blank in the manuscript.*)

4th August[8]

Tears, sweet scents, prayers, flowers.
Oh scatter flowers, white flowers.
On the upturned sod, strew garlands.
Then sing, sing, sing; for I will sleep,
. . . Soft scents like prayers ascend.
Bewail her beloved form now lost from sight . . . .
. . . Your once captive soul, now free . . . .

Gefühl ist alles:
Name ist Schall und Rauch
Umnebelnd Himmelsgluth.

6th August

Silence is to be preferred, for words are profane. Why speak? Of what use are words?
. . . Then, I would not be sincere in my writing. I would emphasize one emotion at the expense of the others. What I felt, what I still feel, cannot be expressed in words. I would involuntarily simulate sad feelings which I have not experienced. But I must not wish to write . . . . Why should I give rigid form to my tenderness? It is much better for my emotion to remain fluid.
Throughout the night I remained motionless, forgetting my body. I was neither sad nor gay. I did not think, but the clarity of my perception was extraordinary.

[8] Mme Emmanuèle died on the night of 31st July; André Walter did not learn of her death until three days later. (Gide's note.)

Towards morning I read my Bible. I went to the piano, but was afraid to play : the melodies were too precise.

Wednesday evening

Meditation after devotional reading, then prayer and the sweet sense of an open heart, the peace and calm of a soul perfectly willing to accept everything on faith. Of what use is anything else? Of what use?

For I love you still even though you have disappeared . . . .

Thursday morning

What I need is a very humble, credulous, completely simple faith. After all, is it absolutely certain that faith is blind and that belief in Jesus is folly? O my God! Is it absolutely certain that one must become blind to see you, and that, by contrast, close examination rules out contemplation?

Thomas became convinced when he sought to convince himself. Why do I keep searching for new doubts? The Jews understood clearly when they asked Jesus, 'If you are the Christ, tell us openly.' And Jesus answered, 'You have said it.'

It is quite simple.

Thursday evening

Hope and charity—a patient, considerate heart—a faithful soul—good will, and wholly pious thoughts.

Psalms—and hope, after prayer, of having a prayer answered.

And meditation—living with meditation, loving meditation, and being overcome by ecstasy . . . .

Friday 9th

My heart leaps up, O God! My heart leaps up. I will sing, I will make my musical instruments ring out.

96

Awaken, my soul. Awaken, lute and harp! I will awaken the dawn!

. . . In you, Lord, I place my trust. I seek a refuge in the shadow of your wings.

. . . I will hope continually and praise Him more and more. He is my salvation and my God.

10th August

Lust of the eyes, lust of the flesh, and pride . . . .

The world and desires of the world pass away . . . . Why should I desire anything else? I would find only new attachments, new sorrows, disappointments—and I would forget the past . . . .

And, when all loved ones have gone, what do you want her to do? Remain faithful.

Sunday

Still I must struggle! O Lord, I thought that I had been delivered. Will this weak flesh never be stilled? Is it not enough for the spirit to be quick?

I must struggle unceasingly.

Then I must follow strict practices and resort to ritual prayers in order to keep my restless flesh occupied. In this way I shall also keep my errant mind from going astray or cavilling, for it is excited by the old ferment of passion. It searches ardours free of compunction; to regulate these ardours, then, I must resort to rational practices.

Calm faith and not sudden bursts of faith.

Monday

Lord—have pity on me. Now everything is lost—have pity on me, a sinner—have pity on me, Lord, have pity on me . . . .

Rather than burn . . . .

But what am I to do? Horrified by such things, I have always shunned them—I know nothing—I am ridiculously ignorant of all that.

Then where? In the street, one of these errant women approaches and leads you away—and there, in her quarters or somewhere else—she gives herself to you, coldly; you pay her, watch what she does. And after all your disgust, you still have desires?

—Yes, a quick embrace which numbs the senses; —but this slow, habitual job!

—Then afterwards—what? Again? Oh, what shame!

Tuesday 13th

Awoke this morning feeling sad and confused; a painful awareness of my wretched state forced itself upon my torpid mind. Songs of yesterday still vibrate in my ears, as if dulled and returned as distant echoes; —and in the nothingness of wrecked dreams, my tears flow painfully, —and as a result of my sin, I am overcome by disgust. *Eripe me de luto.*

And I thought that never again, perhaps, would hopes stir my soul at night in spring . . . .

14th *August* ....
15th *August*[9]..

Friday 16th

And the mountain peaks reappeared.
Lead me to the top of the cliff beyond my reach.

Saturday, 17th August

The work of each will be manifested (I Cor. 3 : 13).

[9] Words crossed out. (Gide's note.)

The work of each! Woe is me!

What am I doing here? Buried in this solitude, lost in the contemplation of my dream—I waste my strength; nothing will come of it all.

My vaulting hopes are sterile! Sterile are the thoughts, struggles, and toil which cause me to lift up my eyes; sterile also is my compassion. My tears flow down my cheeks, comforting no one.

Sterile also is my flesh, voluntarily and laboriously sterile in pursuit of vain chastity.

Useless—wholly useless; having accomplished nothing, accomplishing nothing . . . . O ambitions of yore! Always dreaming of things sublime and never attaining anything.

And now disappointments; so it is—cowardly regrets!

Awaken, you who sleep! And rise up among the dead!

Allain is there. Labour and endure—and look backward no longer . . . .

Saturday evening

I shall not leave this place until I finish my book : I must work on it furiously.

—But how hard it is to recapture a thought which has escaped.

Sunday morning

To keep anything from outside from distracting me, any noise, any sight, I have drawn the curtains across the windows of my room; the lamp lit even during the day to create the illusion of working at night when everything is asleep—no noises, no sights.

To create a calm, comforting atmosphere, I go one step further : clocks and watches are stopped—timelessness. I work in the absolute, apart from time or space. As much food and sleep as I need—the time does not matter, the hour has passed

—and some oil for the lamp, to keep it from going out in the middle of the night.

—No shadows on the walls; darkness is the setting which illuminates a projected thought . . . .

ALLAIN. —Love scheme.
Everything is taking shape.

One soul loves another; they come to resemble each other closely, so closely that they are finally indistinguishable. From the outset they need only a tacit language for communicating with each other; their bodies will hinder them, perhaps, for these bodies will have other desires.

Since the soul is immaterial, it will be capable of existing without things; when the body sleeps, it will escape in dreams—and its soul mate will recognize it even though no one suspects its doing so; then, when the body awakens, reason will call the fugitive back. Here I am thinking of days and nights that have passed—when we were so deeply in love, Emmanuèle. Why speak of your marriage? All of that is now a part of the past; what remains is our love.

Then death set you free. And since the soul is immortal, precious loves will live on. All else has gone, spirit and reason; that which lives on henceforth is your will to love—nothing will hold it back any longer.

Souls better than bodies can join in ecstatic embrace.
I shall be all love and you all tenderness.

(Flaubert)

Thus Allain will first know the soul through the body—then he will love only the soul and dispense with the body. As long as the body lives, love will be constrained, but as soon as death comes, love will triumph over all obstacles.

It is the spirit that gives life, the flesh is of no avail: She dies, *then* he possesses her . . . .

Yes, but Allain still lives : he asks the impossible; the flesh will take revenge. His soul will long for ever closer communion, but carnal lust will interfere—the more sublime the flight of the soul is, the more it will be debased by the flesh.

Doubts arise. The boredom of reality will make him a prisoner of his dream : he will not emerge from his dream.

Madness lies ahead.

HE WILL NOT EMERGE . . . .

—It does not matter. Let us go all the way.

—My mother used to say to me: 'You cannot make your dream come true; but you must find your place in life!'

But suppose you cannot find your place in life! . . .

I have been a fool! You forced me to it (II Cor. 12 : 11).

Monday

—'You cannot make your dream come true.'

It does not matter! You have to struggle: the contest is beautiful even without victory. Hopeless battles are noblest; then the taste of victory resides in the audacity of the undertaking. The soul must rebel against imprisonment: surrender only to oneself and to God . . . and then? Jacob wrestled with the angel —*and was the victor!*—though his flesh was mutilated. That is the way things are. Flesh humbled under a triumphant soul : *The flesh will cry out, but it will submit to the ardour of the spirit.*

Will governs acts, and that is as it should be; but it governs even dreams—that is truly remarkable. Dreams subjected to the will and life in dreams.

I shall not let myself be dominated by anything.

Stronger than life . . . . And than death as well : Love has conquered death, the love of a desirous soul. The flesh alone is mortal; the soul is eternal.

O death, where is thy sting? O grave, where is thy victory?

Because I create you in my dreams. —Power of dreams!

I wish to dominate everything, and solely by the ardour of my soul.

I must be proud.

... *May also be manifested in our mortal flesh* (II Cor. 4 : 11).

We live in order to manifest, not in order to live. —End and means : there is the difference. Morality consists in identifying that which should be sought after for its own sake and the means of attaining it.

Life is merely a means, not an end : I shall not pursue it for its own sake.

We live to manifest; but often involuntarily, unconsciously, and for truths unknown to us, because we are ignorant of the justification for our own existence.

—Then is action necessary?

Martha is active, Mary contemplative; when from their boat Peter and John see Christ on the bank, Peter rushes forward— John remains behind and prays : Mary was the Magdalene, John, the beloved disciple of Christ.

Be comforted, my soul; remember your prayers.

Phenomena are the language of God.

The variety of phenomena is only apparent, their succession in time and space exists only in our minds. Beyond their transient multiplicity appear truths which are unfolded and explained in time and space. We ourselves, when we are only spectators, become involuntary actors in a play whose meaning is unknown to us. We do not know the second signification of our acts; their significance in the realm of the immortal escapes us; they do not stop where we think. —The slightest vibration of a soul reverberates for a long time in the space around it; the faintest shouts evoke distant echoes. The mysterious relations between beings are not altered with impunity; nothing is extinguished, nothing dies once it has begun its existence; everything continues and is propagated to infinity—reverberations spread like waves.

Thus the echo of some primitive song of ecstasy impels my soul towards unknown forms of worship.

Tuesday 20th

The enemy is within us: that is the terrible part. Flight is not possible. You are uneasy, you wander about, you become desperate. —You lock yourself up in your room; the enemy locks himself up with you. —Panic results when you no longer know what to do . . . . Or boundless sadness, cowardly surrender, a desire to end it all.

Sin is lying at the door; its desire is for you, but you must master it (Gen. 4:7).

Wednesday

One of the worst forms of anguish results from not knowing; no one guides me, counsels me, comforts me.

Not knowing whether the desired goal is humanly possible— ignorant of everything, of evil and remedies. Struggling alone against an unknown enemy!

I wrote:

'Oh! Oh! The salt of the earth!

'I abhor myself! *But if the salt have lost its savour* . . . .

'I would like above all to avoid the caresses of others and friendly words which show me that they do not understand. And I suffer from their mistake as much as from the solitude of my evil. —And no one knows!

'Oh! To suffer in solitude! . . .

'Regeneration has seemed impossible, for I have to hide my protracted struggle from everyone; still I have felt certain that a friendly word would help me, sustain me in my struggle . . .

'But I walk through life always with a smile; I talk, joke, play my role because no one must suspect the agony of my soul which feels that it is dying, dying completely.

'I contain with my sad studies, feel time escaping in the stupid task of a man who seems to have several lives ahead of him, thinking that tomorrow, perhaps, everything will come to an end, sink into darkness. Oh! To die completely. Pity, Lord!

'So many songs still run through my tired brain! If only I could shout . . . and be heard!'

I continued writing:

'What would I not give to learn whether others, those whom I love, have suffered as I from the evil which torments me. —Oh! No! I should have seen it in their look, I should have felt it in their words . . . . They would not speak of these things as they do, offhandedly; they would not laugh as they do! . . .

'That is why I should like, in this book, to give voice to what I have in my heart—for myself alone—or perhaps, if any exists, for those who suffer the anguish that I have suffered and who like me despair, thinking that they are alone in their suffering.

'And I should like to punish, with all my strength, those who treat chastity as folly; who scoff at virtue, as if it were a weakness . . . .

'I must dare to say these things.'

Child that I was, thinking that everything could be said! —But the words did not even exist. Language is only for ordinary emotions; extreme emotions are lost in the attempt to reveal them. Always excessive in all things, how could I speak? If I could speak, why should I? They would not understand—They would say: 'He is a fool', laugh, shrug their shoulders, and turn away . . . . I am not lacking in courage, but I might grieve some of the faint-hearted who are dear to me, and in the eyes of many my action would be scandalous . . . . Still, I have these things in my soul; others seek to ignore them: it seems to them that in this way they are suppressing them.

So I fall silent, withdraw into myself, smile at others; they prefer a mask; after a short while, they believe that the mask is reality!

> *and take refuge in solitude*
> *and surrender to despair ....*

The first stirrings, the first spontaneous outbursts of the soul are easy; easy, too, the first ecstasies! How many who have known them now curse them!

But a faith recaptured after its abandonment, reconstructed after its destruction by doubt . . . a faith which reason ridicules, which the flesh abuses, and which pride, sensing its imprisonment, spitefully resists—this faith is noble, conscious of its existence, voluntary; hence its superiority.

ASCETIC PRACTICES

—But such a demon is overcome only by prayer and fasting.

Let the spirit rule constantly, never losing its footing for even an instant; as long as it is steadfast, the flesh is submissive—but do not let it weaken—*Watch and pray that you may not succumb to temptation.* At night, when hallucinations appear . . . O Luther, throwing his inkpot at the marauding demon!

Thursday 22nd

Mortify the deeds of the body.

The coarse hair of the cilice voluptuously arouses the soul; fasting produces giddiness bordering on ecstasy; ardour—and when the flesh weakens, then cold water and damp linens flagellate weak loins; and then, nerves torn to shreds, body calm, overwhelmed by grief—oh! Sleep at last in the form of a divine dream.

You will not be the victor unless you do violence to yourself
(*Imitation of Christ* I : 22).

23rd August

No matter! This struggle in darkness—all alone, body to body —is sublime, and pride sometimes whispers arrogant exultations after the victory. When it is not debasing, this struggle is strangely edifying; it is the sovereign proof which consumes or magnifies.

How proud am I, Lord, that you have judged me worthy!

Sunday 25th

O Lord! I am pure! I am pure! I am pure! I am pure!

Monday 26th

The Spirit shakes its chains so violently that it breaks them or is broken by them. Heaven tempts it, and the inaccessible; it dreams of ever more sublime flights; oblivious of its fetters, it surges upward . . . . And feathers flutter in the spirit's wake, torn from its great wings, and fall to the earth.

The fluttering feathers, spattered with blood and tears—these melodious feathers are songs.

Oh! They long for nobility! They advocated lofty life: *Sursum corda*, they say. But noble souls, in the final analysis, are not born to live; life repels them; they are doomed from the start.

Fortunately they are few in number, for they perish.

> *Your men depart, O Eternal One,*
> *God of battles, the valiant fall.*

— But first his wings must be clipped; this is simply a barnyard fowl.

And his spirit will not be overcome by *Spirit*, which might give rise to self-glorification, or by the angel of Jacob.

His spirit will be overcome by unchaste Thecla, for *God chose the lowly things of this world to confound the wise.*

'You must struggle *continuously.*' I know the words *continuous* and *continual—continually*, yes, but continuously? I am not sure. I need a dictionary . . . .

Dolorously—emphatic, too Spanish—external—not intimate —must use *dolorously,* which expresses sorrow much more discreetly.

Wednesday 28th

Something more breathless, loud, fortuitous—so much the worse! Then I can choose; I have too many 'pieces' here. I am trying too hard to know myself: I must concentrate more on self-analysis.

Yes—cries of passion, even though the sentences are not perfect—I want the angles, breaks, rough edges to remain—and without having to worry about explaining to someone who has failed to understand immediately: synthetic, no matter what D*** may say.

Then let the new emotion guide me instead of my forcing it into a preconceived frame.

Subject, Verb, Attribute.

One must always come back to this inevitable relation. But it is unsatisfactory: not everything evidences such an inexorable dependence; there are more subtle correlations.

This rough syntax focuses attention on them; a hint is sufficient.

Pas la couleur, rien que la nuance.

It is in the relation between words, no longer in the sentence as a whole:

Kühl bis ans Herz hinein . . . .

Connection between two essences—perfect.

But better still alliterative rhythm, undulation of complete and rounded sentences—and the interrupted reminder of assonances.

And when stubborn syntax protests, it must be subdued—for to subject thought to syntax would seem to me to be a cowardly act. One must not give in to things.

> *Et pour sa voix lointaine, et calme, et grave, elle a*
> *L'inflexion des voix chères qui se sont tues.*[10]

That is something prose cannot do : caesuras are violated in a normal scansion; underneath a refractory appearance, the rule which has nevertheless been followed, brings out the fantastic rhythm.

> *. . . et calme, et grave, elle a*

These light and dark alliterations, repeated three times, create the impression of slow footsteps traversing infinite space; then beginning with the last two words, the movement is regular, without even a caesura, as if the whole constituted a fourteen syllable verse . . . .

> *. . . elle a*
> *L'inflexion des voix chères qui se sont tues.*

It is the infinite line of horizons glimpsed after death, glimpsed fleetingly in HER words.

Midnight

I was playing the piano—and every string was vibrating; but

[10] Verlaine's 'Mon rêve familier' may have appealed to Gide for another reason. The verses quoted suggest possession through memory and idealization.

the vibrations were too strong, and suddenly one string broke. —I stopped, terrified by the piercing sound of the metallic string. It stopped vibrating, but for a long time the most distant harmonies resounded as if moved by grief, like a harmonious wave surging over a whole gamut of notes. Then the ethereal subsided as it spread. —Everything again fell silent. The silence which had been broken for an instant again enveloped me in fear and solitude.

I was still trembling, afraid of rekindling the sorrow expressed by the mute keyboard over the death of the note. I tried to read, to dream—and now that I am writing, in the darkness I keep hearing a sob—from a lute with a broken string.

Since we are surrounded by so great a crowd of witnesses (Heb. 12 : 1).

METAPHORICAL: HUGO.
Invisible lights surround us in what we believe to be dark night; souls light up like candles, souls already dead or souls not yet born; immaterial space is vibrant with lights—and man is surrounded by infinite legions arranged in an ascending hierarchy extending to God . . . .

(Too much illumination, rhetoric, words outweighing thoughts—in relation to man—must cultivate penumbras in which the mysterious is vaguely sensed.)

SYMBOLIC . . . . *On an azure field, great angels bent in contemplation . . . .*

For souls, too, there are laws of resonance. The quivering of a single soul immediately disturbs all surrounding souls capable of perfect unison. Vibrations of subtle chords agitate them; they are in a constant harmonious relationship—perhaps even a mathematical relationship—each of them produces a distinct sound, for each has its own harmonies. And these harmonies allow God to identify them : like the purest crystal, the most exquisite soul has pellucid sounds.

And that explains why we sometimes are moved by mysterious manifestations of tenderness : an isolated chord in the air causes our soul to vibrate; a tenuous song, imperceptible, awakens some latent alliteration in the soul.

Friday 30th

There must be a Providence; a God is not sufficient; he must see you. That is still not sufficient : he must love; afterwards, everything else is the same. Everything is sacrificed in its turn; love of duty can ruin happiness; I become virtuous, sublime; only a very few need know it—only you alone, even if you are dead—I can still accept this condition; absolute self-sacrifice, but I want God at least to remain, the last refuge after everything else has failed—and I want God to see me and bless my efforts; otherwise life embraces only nothingness—and this insight is a cry of terror from the heart of darkness :

Eternal One! Eternal One! How many times have I cried out to you as a child cries out to his father, and you have not answered.

Three stages of ecstasy :

> *Last night my hands were taut but not tired;*
> *My soul refuses all consolation;*
> *I remember God and I groan;*
> *I meditate and my spirit is depressed.*

Eternal One! Lord! Oh! Reveal yourself! I remain kneeling for a long time, and my body becomes restless as my soul searches for new expressions for its prayers, and is sometimes startled by its eternal monologue. —Oh! To hear no response; to *believe* always; faith without anything to reassure you; —to wait, pray, and know already that hope is deceptive—and to keep on praying, in spite of everything, because perhaps . . . .

First alternative: . . .

Either, when the soul succeeds in being deceived by dreams, the body becomes despondent because it is unable to embrace anything and gives in to its grief. —*Noli me tangere* . . . I cannot, Lord! I must touch you; my whole body longs for you; desire torments me; my arms reach out into the night only to enfold nothingness; I wring my hands in despair . . . have pity on me: I am so miserable!

Second alternative: Or prayer illuminates and I cover my eyes with my hands to keep anything from interfering with the divine dream; I feel God near me . . . then suddenly I turn around and feel that I am alone—the feeling that all of this is a lugubrious mockery . . . but no! I want to start over, to enter again into the state of ecstasy—I pray more fervently, aloud: but doubt appears, irony, my spirit languishes, my nerves grow taut, and the prayer dies on stammering lips. —Well, that is all for tonight; I have to sleep without God; it is two o'clock. Oh! How my head tires from searching always for the Invisible! —And now tears . . . and reason which whispers derisively to the soul, saying: 'You did not have to pray so long; that bores me.'

ALLAIN

He asks of religion more than it can offer him; this causes him to waver and to doubt:

—Doubt even in a state of ecstasy:

'and remain kneeling, no longer knowing . . . etc . . . .'

INFLUENCE OF FOOD ON RELIGIOUS STATES—

ARTIFICIAL ECSTASY. MEDDLESOME FLESH OB-
LIGED—NERVOUS CAUSES.

(to be completed)

But also what joy when ecstasy finally comes, the sweet reward
for perseverance; when adoration follows prayer; when, after a
night of struggling I fall asleep in the morning, lulled by an
orational refrain.

1st September

Allain thinks:

'Emmanuèle is not the only one; my mother also and Lucie,
the souls of all my loved ones surround me and contemplate
me.'

He is gladdened by the thought. He peoples his solitude with
intimate friends who have passed on.

Let this thought sustain him.

Father! I desire, wherever I am, to have with me those whom
you have given to me— Oh! To be worthy! To feel, after the
victory of battles, their gentle smile illuminate the shadows. To
be valiant so that they may rejoice and afterwards, later on,
say to me:

You have fought a good fight—God has found you faithful—
in all things.

Monday 2nd

Last night, looking into the mirror, I contemplated my image.
As if it has emerged from darkness, the fragile apparition takes
shape and becomes rigid; the dimly lighted shadows around me
grow darker. My eyes penetrate these eyes: and my soul hovers
uncertainly between this double illusion, dazed, and wondering
which is the reflection of the other and whether *I* am not an
image, an unreal phantom; wondering which of the two is look-

ing at the other and sensing its identity. My eyes penetrate his, and in the depth of *his* pupils I search for *my* thought . . . .

Allain threw a large cloth over the image, imprisoning it; I no longer see it—but I feel that it is still alive under the cloth, behind the glass; afraid of its look, I dare not lift the veil and I feel it looking at me when I turn around; it is a breath between my shoulders.

Exasperated, he will crush it—but he is held back by fear of splitting the phantom and causing nothingness to appear behind the broken illusion.

HALLUCINATION: TAINE.

It is enough for nerve centres to be shattered; they are no longer shattered by the senses, by external perception—but by the inner will which, through them, creates the image.

For a long time it labours, toils without success, for it is too self-conscious and rids itself of the notion of effort only with great difficulty; but suddenly, unexpectedly, as a result of the habit established over a long period of time through an association provoked artificially at first and now natural—the image emerges spontaneously.

Veiled in darkness, at dusk, I have seen you leaning on the head of my bed, like a shadow, silent. Your head rested on your hand, as if tired—it was covered with a pall.

I became frightened, and the vision vanished.

Thursday 5th

Un baiser doux et savoureux
Ai pris de la rose erramment.
Moult est gueri qui tel fleur baise;
Et cependant j'ai maint ennui
Souffert et mainte male nuit,
Depuis qu'ai la rose baisée.

The memory of your caress torments me.

It was in the evening, by the piano, you came to listen to me—and then your hand, your cool hand, softly caressed my brow—why?

This evening is so pleasant, I weep; the caress of the breeze has reminded me of your caress; the memory of your hand on my brow has made my soul quake.

Friday 6th

White cloak, white hood . . . and who knows the agitation inherent in this heart that is for ever sealed, this life that is for ever mute? Everything involves only the man and God; outsiders have no hint of these sublime struggles and supreme ardours.

The Carthusians have prayed; then comes death; they are at rest.

Now the vigil; it is midnight; in the lighted chapel, beneath the dark arches of the cloister, the Carthusians sing canticles. O holy peace of monasteries! Repose of convents! Peace of cloisters!

Happy he who kneels down and has not struggled.

Monday 9th

Get up early: dawn is radiant—vivacity of morning prayers. Go to bed late: the calm of night is comforting—ecstasy of silent hours.

To avoid boredom on dismal afternoons, lie down during the day, when the heat is overwhelming. Or fall asleep towards evening and awaken with a start, in the middle of the night, when the clock strikes; get up, kneel immediately; prayer is pure then, for the spirit, dulled by dreams, puts aside doubt; read, work, wait for morning to come, and, when morning comes, quietly fall asleep.

That is what I have done these three last nights; when I went to bed, the sky was pink.

Wednesday

Only sight is deceived; sometimes hearing—but when I seek to touch, the vision vanishes.

Not to be able to seize your shadow! I am frightened by this solitude; my heart and soul are pierced as if by a cold shudder of absent caresses. Oh! I would like to snuggle close to you, sit at your feet, be enveloped by your warmth, my head on your knees, in the deep folds of your dress, and to feel the sweet warmth of your breath on my brow.

Thursday 12th

Oh! Speak to me, my love! I am all alone, you know—and have nothing to guide me except my faith, which is always giving in to exhaustion. I live on memories and hope, never having anything to rekindle love except the ardour of my faithful soul.

Oh! Speak! So that I may know!

Nocturnal hours

In the darkness, leaning out the window, gasping for air! Oh! I am suffocating—air! Oh! I have a fever—cold air! To cool my feverish lungs. My head burns; oh! My brow is pressed against the pane and the palm of my hands against the wet stones. Oh! I breathe.

Melancholy calm of outstretched night, after the sweating and panting of flesh—the lull.

Prepare the night for dreams—you, my silent friend, with your silent rays streaming through the clouds.

—Prepare the night for new delights—you, my distant friend, as you line each cloud with silver.

—Prepare the night for more ecstatic states—for enchantment rather than appeasement—by your silences—stillness—ethereal brightness.

Then I would be lulled to sleep by your harmonies.

In the darkness, leaning out of the window, I contemplate the boundless night, the wan sorcery of shadows cast by romantic moonlight.
When the soul discovers . . . .

Silence.—

When the soul learned the truth, it cried out:
'I curse you again, wretched flesh! Curses on you! Curses on you!

Then it lamented the fact that it no longer found words for prayer—and was equally grieved because the words would have to come from the same lips which had so longed for bittersweet embraces. Words are sullied as they are spoken; prayer no longer ascends.

The soul speaks:
'Behold! Behold! I have lost you again, sweet white purity, arduously reclaimed anew. Gone are your promises, gone are your loving memories. Gone! Gone!'

Then self-recrimination:
'But you were also negligent, errant one! Always being led astray by your idle dreams! You should have stayed near your body and stood guard. —Shame on you. Repent and cry like a coward.'

And the soul deplored its plight and wept because it was conscious of its wretchedness.

Saturday 14th

I have prayed all night, kneeling, without turning around. I do not dare to sleep—O dread of dismal darkness! Grief of departed visions. Terror of witnesses invoked in the past. —Hide . . . O their wrathful gaze directed at the weak worldling! How sad is their gaze! How sad! —The peace of their wrinkled brows . . . .

All night long I have wept: my tears are pious; I proffer only the prayer of one who has sinned greatly and feels ashamed.

O tears which fall in darkness . . . .

He is terrified by the host of demons summoned by his invocation.

'Eternal One! Have pity on me! I fear the darkness! All the loved ones who peopled my long vigils have departed—they have left me all alone; they have deserted me. I fear the darkness; silence harbours countless imaginary fears. I dare not turn around; I am afraid! I am afraid, Lord—Oh! I am a child! A little child!' He sobs.

. . . Because she does not possess the full light and all of her affections are unsound (Imitation of Christ III: 55).

I have to work.

15th September

The pattern is always the same. The spirit soars; it forgets to keep watch: the flesh falls. I awaken; then comes a tremendous effort to rid myself of wicked thoughts. The struggle exhausts me, I say to myself: 'What is the use?' I pray, pursue ecstasy— and the cycle begins anew.

When I have completed the cycle several times, there are no more surprises: it is hopeless. It is not a circle, however, it is an ever widening spiral whose rings diverge further and further from the centre; leaps are more abrupt; surges more frenzied.

Monday 16th

He thinks:

Rousseau worked eighteen hours—

Balzac from midnight to eight o'clock—
Flaubert . . . etc.

He tries to stay awake—the flesh is weak . . . (admirable):
sleep overcomes him even as he resists—he falls asleep with his
elbow on the table . . . .

'heavy, heavy head.'

The body will say:
*Behold! Bring us back to Egypt! There we ate succulent
onions, there we lived a life of plenty; but you cause us to wander
in an arid, waterless desert, where we have nothing and suffer
from many things.*

. . . the plaintive flesh senses the restless echo of past delights
still suggested by some provocative refrain—and in spite of everything, the corruptive image emerges.

Tuesday evening

Metaphysical thoughts.

Time and space exist only in the mind of man. Study these
profundities and contemplate them until you feel dizzy. Slow
charm of past sadnesses—present grief, think of it as already far
in the past, see yourself without thinking 'It is I suffering', and
change it into an exquisite sadness, a memory of grief . . . the
illusion of phenomena. For death is only an accident to minds
that survive; but as soon as death comes the soul, no longer per-
ceiving it, forgets death, for memories of times past depart with
the deceased mind. The soul overleaps death, indifferent.

That which changes is the body alone: it returns to dust—
(again phenomenally). Death is not an end; the book does not
stop there. Who knows where it stops? . . . And whether it begins
with life? —Who knows whether it even begins? —Whether the
soul is not eternally wandering, effecting uneasy migrations,
across an unending series of fleeting forms and multiple lives, in

an attempt to manifest its essence? . . . Perhaps its infinite lassitude is caused by all these former lives; or perhaps it is still very young, and that causes its boundless yearnings.

Oh! When we know! Oh! When we see the light! *For until this day the same veil remains unlifted. —But then shall we know even as we are known.*

Yes! But when we know, we shall no longer have a reason to know, or to desire; we shall know without suspecting, without the magical element of surprise, without awareness. This will be the resolution of a chord held in suspension too long, without our having ears to hear it; and we shall no longer have eyes to view the dazzling spectacle of brilliant flashes ascending. We shall be plunged into infinite happiness, with no more of this grievous resistance of the self which alone could cause us to sense it.

Alternative : a prodigious nirvana, a state in which the 'self' is totally lost in ecstasy even as it retains voluntary consciousness of its swoon; this would be a voluptuously perceptible nothingness.

Abstract speculations : pursuing the wind, chasing chimeras— Oh the mirage, during life, of things beyond life . . . .

Wednesday 18th

Above all, ardour must not diminish—otherwise everything will collapse immediately; I must not even dream of it for fear that the thought of the nothingness of all life will tantalize my soul, —but must keep it burning always with the incessant desire for new ecstasies.

Thursday

I am working excessively : Allain is progressing; it is superb! Then each day sees the birth of some new projects which I would like to write immediately—some philosophical stories, especially, then the treatise on *Refuges*—the poem on *The Wandering Jew* . . . .

My thoughts are so tumultuous that the pain of falling asleep is almost physical. It is like a cessation of being; only the idea is insufferable. Each day I delay the moment of retiring—and as soon as darkness reigns, I experience insufferable anguish; I no longer wish to fall asleep, and my reason says that I must; gradually my thoughts stop, slow down—are on the point of dying, but sudden surges of life agitate them once more; my mind is painfully aware that it is slowly being overpowered, and is horrified. Or it is beset by nerve-racking obsessions.

Nights will come when I shall search for sleep without finding it.

Music: only Schumann and Bach—(Wagner is too overwhelming). Obsession with numbers.

In Bach, obstinate fugues—in Schumann, stubborn rhythms which brutalize measures and persist in spite of beats; anguish results. —The bass notes resort to syncopation, the alto notes split, and when the two harmonize, a painful lassitude results.

Sunday

Here is how it begins.

In the silence of the night, as soon as I blow out the candle and lie down, what comes is not sleep but a melody, a short melody, simple and susceptible of being treated as a fugue. At first it develops simply, then, when repeated, it emerges as an echo, an auxiliary melody which develops in the form of a canon parallel to the first; then a third melody is interwoven in the third measure . . . a fourth tries to emerge; it joins in unison with the first, but its timbre is different; I separate them—they hasten on —everything blends together. —A new beginning. —The first melody chances a flourish; the second follows; then the third— the first speeds up—the others follow, taking the form of a scherzo . . . . Soon it becomes an unbearable obsession; I arise, and in order to put an end to it, I strike chords on the piano at random—and the disturbing melody resounds loudly when it crashes into the chords that I have struck, creating a REAL dissonance.

—Or a chromatic progression which arises inexorably, in spite of my efforts, through whole scales.

Each night comes a new obsession.

Yesterday—a vague, fleeting progression which went through all the registers and reached inadmissible heights; it kept ascending even after it should have dropped down quickly to a lower note in order to begin a new ascent—but where? For it seems continuous—and my attentive ear seeks to identify the precise note on which the backward leap will occur; the progression goes too quickly, rushing furiously onward—I try to stop it— I cling to it—finally it carries me away with it in a stuporous state : sleep has come.

Double rhyme—the last verse to have irregular metre and the two preceding syllables fluctuating, like the uncertain stop of a swing which is moved upward by a forward thrust but must soon reverse its course. To give the impression of branches swaying in a breeze.

Sleep, Sleep.

Willows, osiers, encircle full my brow,
Spread your branches, moved slowly to and fro
   By a breath, oh so gentle now;
Beneath the dark mystery of your leaves,—throw
   The caresses of your shades.

I suffer, long for sleep; sweet babbling flow
Of waters, sing softly, sing at will,
   Waters of brooks, murmuring low.

My soul hears, forgetful of time—the still
Flight of hours, eternally.

I would fall asleep, my dear, in your embrace,
To the distant memory of your first vow;
Silence! Do not speak; but place
Your hand, your cool hand in mine; —how
In dream I bid your shadow come.

'Throw' is an unhappy choice; its brusqueness excludes the
following caress.

Tuesday 24th

In order to describe it correctly in Allain, I must observe in
myself the delicate moment when my thoughts become dis-
ordered. The distinctive trait of this . . .[11] is that it is not per-
ceived; still, by a conscious effort of will, it must be made perceptible. —In the silence and darkness of the night, I have
followed the chain of my thoughts—it is very strange. Beginning
with an aphorism, I let my thoughts wander freely; then, when
I come to an observation which amuses me, I re-examine, idea
by idea, the thin thread which relates and speciously connects
the initial aphorism with the last observation. Next I manage
to follow, at the same time, two chains of thought; then mental
associations are most strange: the two systems of connected
ideas preserve their relationship as they evolve.

Wednesday

Now I know! The spirit becomes morbid . . . (study).
He no longer wishes to pursue the idea; all along the way, he
mumbles lines, verses with periodic alliterations . . . and then,
when he wishes to attempt to track down the idea, he no longer

[11] Word omitted. (Gide's note.)

remembers what he was thinking. —An impression of tracking down empty space—but, afterwards, utter exhaustion.

In the woods, Friday

The spirit must rest.

Last night, almost unable to sleep because my brain was too active, I dreamed of long journeys, of extreme fatigue; and in a dream filled with visions, golden fields were unfolded, and slopes of valleys cooled by a stream which moved swiftly through its willow-shaded channel. And in the stream I saw again the thin torsos and sun-tanned limbs of the children from . . . they were swimming and diving in these cold surroundings. —I became furious because I was not one of them, not one of these vaga-bonds who bask in the sun by day and lie down at night in a ditch, unmindful of the cold or rain; and when they are feverish, they dive, stark naked, into the refreshing coolness of streams . . . . And who do not think.

So I was on my way by five o'clock this morning; I walked along a stream which mirrored huge rocks and tall trees in a forest extending beyond the range of sight; everything was drowned in a humid mist which gave everything a bluish hue and conferred on the valley a tempting and mysterious depth. The sun was still hidden by this outstretched haze; the earth seemed to float on a cloud. I was maddened by the soft caress of the air; I walked along as in a state of delirium; my acute senses almost frightened me by their extraordinary vibrations: colours stroked me and wounded me, as if by contact.

I started to run under low branches heavy with dew; as I passed underneath them, sparkling droplets splashed on my brow. I moved like a drunkard; my ears hummed with the orchestrated sounds of the mighty *Scherzo in C Minor*.

The forest opened, higher, more solemn; underneath thick boughs I found the cool atmosphere of a cavern, the contem-plative mood of a cathedral. Boundless longings surged through my soul and brought to my lips verses which I recited aloud. I found melancholic enchantment in my solitude, peopling it with my loved ones; before my eyes appeared, vaguely at first, the supple forms of children playing on the beach, children whose beauty haunts me; I would have liked to bathe also, near them, and to have felt the softness of their brown skin. But I was all alone; then I was overpowered by a violent shudder, and I mourned the imperceptible flight of my dream . . . .

. . . walking all the way to the edge of the sea.

Saturday, Le P***

All day long I had made them laugh, hilariously. Then evening came; I went back alone to my room. I sat down, my spirit listless.

Everything was calm; I thought that I was alone in my vigil; it was midnight. The light was out; the wind outside was blowing towards the sea; then the utter artificiality of this joy brought on a feeling of disgust: sorrow overwhelmed me. Lulled by my languid sadness, I buried my head under the cover and cried like a child. I was delirious, I think; I felt thoughts descending on me like gusts of wind on fields of wheat, and they caused my head to sway so violently that I was afraid of becoming insane.

Then I arose and walked around in my room; I was barefoot; I felt a shiver come over me, a delightful shiver. Gusts moved across the sea and the wind howled in the corridor. I looked outside: everything was wrapped in a pall of gloom. As far as the eye could see, everything was colourless. The sea surged nearby, and the shore and waves were grey, though the grey was vanishing in the dusk. It was sad, as if the dead sun had transferred its grief to things. —Oh! The pall of twilight!

And the waves discussed the dead rays and departed flashes of light in voices that seemed to come from beyond the tomb.

My heart was paralysed by boredom.

Monday 30th

That is all a ridiculous waste of time—and it brings me no repose. I can no longer sleep. —I must work faster.

1st October

ALLAIN. —The work must be completed. —But madness is imminent.

I am caught in a dilemma—

Rest? —I would be losing ground—and I would not thwart its advance;—besides, I cannot rest.

Speed up, then! Press furiously onward with the task—but this hastens its arrival.

There is no way out.

Too bad! —It will be a mad race.

3rd October

Oh! To leave something behind—not to die completely; my notebook, then, if Allain is not completed or if I lose my mind too soon.

I write it formally here:

LET PIERRE C***, TO WHOM I GIVE THEM, PUBLISH THESE NOTEBOOKS IF I BECOME MAD—WITHOUT CONCERN FOR MY POSTHUMOUS MEMORY ... UNLESS THEY DO NOT ALREADY SEEM TOO INSANE —I LET HIM BE THE JUDGE.

A white notebook, a black notebook as she would have wished. I thought about using Besnard's aquarelles, which you liked so well, but there is no other way, it seems. And then that will be all.

IF HE PUBLISHES MY NOTEBOOKS—HE SHOULD KEEP ALLAIN: ONE OR THE OTHER.

And I thank him for it.

4th October

The race to madness—which of the two will arrive first, Allain or I? I place my wager on Allain; I hold back, restrain myself; I rush, speed up the work, press on the dénouement of Allain : I must make him lose his mind before I become mad. Which of the two will win out over the other? —The race is very amusing; I play all the roles myself, gambler, fighter, adversary. —The prize will be rest, rest after the work is finished. Will you not bless me, God? —Otherwise I shall have lost everything, you see, because I loved duty too much, because I wanted to remain faithful—and because I struggled. Will you not give me your hidden manna, God, and the white raiment which you reserve for the pure? The seraphim will say : 'Why is he so pale? He has the strange eyes of a visionary!'—and You, You will answer : 'He has fought the good fight—give him the palm of glory.'

Sunday

Ridiculous feelings of tenderness for unknown creatures met in the country—for a child at rest . . . simple happiness . . . . *The waters of Shiloh flow gently.*

I must not go out any longer, or only at night.

Monday 7th

I grow drowsy towards evening, am obsessed by reverie; I awaken in the sultry night; I go out, walk until the moon sets; return; I feel alone, and my soul trembles.

And then, until morning, I remain trembling, my mind blank, and I lie down only at daybreak, because I dare not fall asleep —and because I am afraid—of everything that I cannot see in the darkness.

The Black Notebook

Wednesday night

Three beats to the measure; quarter notes; a succession of four notes, so that the fourth falls on the first beat of the next measure and transfers the initial note to the second beat. I keep on anyway; now it is on the third—again on the first. —I start over.

Four beats to the measure; a succession of five notes. —I calculate: five times four, twenty; then twenty notes and five measures to return to the point of departure.

I start over.

Seven notes and three beats; twenty-one in all . . . .

I have to do this for hours at night, instead of sleeping—and the obsession turns into a nightmare.

Thursday night

My thoughts shift like the deck of a ship pitching in heavy seas—they turn somersaults, fall from dizzying heights, leap upward again. And the vision, as in certain dreams which precede true sleep, of a rising and falling swing—and the impression, with each sudden upward leap, of something coming loose in my head. This rocking motion is so exhausting that I go out and walk in the darkness—bareheaded, dew on my burning brow; but the heavens are so vast that I grow dizzy—

I have to walk until morning to find a few moments of sleep.

Midnight

O speak to me, I beg of you—Elsa, Elsa! My loneliness overwhelms me, maddens me. I people it with chimeras, but I remain terrifyingly alone. —Speak to me . . . .

Nights in particular are terrifying, long; sleepless nights . . . when fear casts a pall around me, when I tremble like a child, and I cry.

. . . or at the organ, slowly, to fill my troubled idleness,

religious sarabands with solemn rhythm and restful sonorities—
until I am frightened by the very sound, lost like me in mute
loneliness . . . .

Souls are lonely!
Souls are lonely!

Sunday

J'ai voulu . . . te rapporter des roses.
Mais j'en avais tant pris dans mes ceintures closes,
Que les nœuds trop serrés n'ont pu les contenir.
Les nœuds ont éclaté, les roses envolées
Par le vent à la mer s'en sont toutes allées.
Elles ont suivi l'eau pour ne plus revenir.

And Schopenhauer whom I have not finished. The fourth book
in its entirety!
So much the worse! I detest pessimism—one must be cheerful
in spite of everything.

Oh! Oh! The epitaph:

HERE LIES ALLAIN WHO BECAME MAD
BECAUSE HE THOUGHT HE HAD A SOUL.

and the verse:
We are fools for Christ's sake (I Cor. 4 : 10).

Tuesday

This morning I was seated . . . it is very amusing. —As caged
birds fly through an open window—I do not know what par-
tition was suddenly broken down, I saw vagabond thoughts flying
away; they were like visions which appeared light against a dark
background . . . not like the cherished images I usually call up—
no, I felt certain that they were departing and would never

return . . . . At first they went away very slowly; I felt the sadness of a farewell; I recognized them all: remembered landscapes, friendly gestures, smiles. —I would have liked to keep them; but, despite the sorrow I felt because of their flight, I remained inert, amused by the spectacle.

Then they rushed out tumultuously, great scraps of life which would light up suddenly and then leap into the darkness . . . .

ALLAIN

He reflects on the IMMATERIAL FORM (melody) under which she can be INTUITIVELY PERCEPTIBLE to his soul (Berlioz).

Rittardendo

. . . ! . . . ! *I shall have loved you well.*

There should be three syllables—the feeling is then one of infinite sadness.

Gajo

. . . *Des aubépines toutes blanches; je t'en cueillerai des branches fleuries.*

Friday?

Strange dreams:

Your existence now? Only in me: you live because I dream of you, when I dream of you, and only then; hence your immortality.

Dear soul, how sweet that you live only by virtue of my living love!

It is through me that you live, through me! Because I love you! . . .

And as your love also fills my thoughts, it is your love, only your love, that causes me to live:

I live only through your love.

It is through you that I live, through you! Because you love me!

You live only when I dream of you and I live only through your love. Does this not mean that I live only when I dream of your love?

If I ceased to love you, you would cease to live—we would both die if we ceased to think of each other. Now I understand, I understand why my love fills my soul completely: it is the condition of our being; we cannot cease to love each other; our love is immortal and beyond our power, for only the death of the soul can destroy it. We shall always exist, one in the desirous thoughts of each other; we exist only through each other; we exist only through our mutual relationship.

I have to love you without ceasing.

In the evening
Now mystic chords from lofty summits spill;
Now from dark woodlands soft caresses fill
The night, perfumed by fragrant flowers;
From lips unknown pour words more fragrant still . . . .

'A faint light which I could not see would illuminate my table' . . . and I watch the pale stars sink into the distance. —I would sing, without this silence; but when all is still, I listen—night, vast night . . . . *Hear, my beloved* . . . .

It is your caress, this pervasive perfume—tell me, it is your caress! —Your harmonious form, like a broken chord, has come apart; it was a random harmony.

What brightness on the hill—I wait—see! The moon—and patches of fog are lined with silver.

Last night I saw escaped visions, visions from the past, vanishing. Memories depart; I have watched their flight. Memories of the past, beloved forms; when all of them depart, the night will be black. Images speed through the star-strewn sky; when all of them depart, I shall be able to sleep.

The life to come might bring new loves—why? —Like the Wandering Jew, I might travel through life, bearing in my heart the silent grief of all those who remained behind—and yet I might have smiles for all the chance companions met on the way, and I might love them, and since everything vanishes, new attachments might replace the old ones? . . . Oh! Why?

And when, later, in spite of everything, still remembering my former loves, children might see me weeping—what could I possibly say to them? They will not have known *them* and will never know the cause of our tears.

Then they might also weep, later, when I left them; and as torn sympathy always leaves a painful wound in each heart, in their turn they might grieve for me silently as I grieved for others. And I might leave them, bearing with me remorse for causing them to love me in spite of myself, and inconsolable grief for leaving them behind.

Having learned, therefore, that all suffering comes from an attachment—he escapes into solitude. —Remain faithful— UNTO DEATH . . . . Let thought sleep—eternally—feel it grow drowsy—the brief moment when thought comes to an end; DEATH. For a long time, I have tried to think of nothing : the idea is finally grasped, intuitively . . . .

—How clear is the night; moths fly around the lamp, and the lamp singes their wings; drawn to the light, the nocturnal butterflies fall, painfully seared.

—How calm. The night compels contemplation. The whisper of the breeze is scarcely heard through the moist leaves. All is still. I search the night for falling stars . . . .

I shall not sleep—the shadows are too beautiful.

Sunday morning

Bluffy—the name of a glacier, an avalanche, a blue stream falling against white snow.

. . . Try to believe—and then mourn—and then again.

Monday

The mysterious moment which precedes true sleep, when the senses, barely lulled to sleep, still have vague perceptions—when reality merges with dream. The last image seen before the eyes close still remains but is oddly and disconcertingly deformed.

Her gaze the other evening was so piercing that I suffered from it as from a sword; and I wanted to turn away from it, but it followed me everywhere. Then her smile became that of a wax doll. It was frightening: I saw all her teeth, between her lips, separated by ridiculous gaps. I wanted to push her away, but my outstretched hand made holes in her; her whole body was full of sand; it emptied itself like a sack. And I lost hope as her deflated body assumed heartrending postures and collapsed.

Oh! When will the night come? . . .

Oh! When will the night come? A pause in time
To bring reprieve from thought and memory.
Dreamless, moonless night, eclipsing peace sublime.

Oh! When will the night come? One to entrance
As slowly as it makes timid advance,
Urging surrender to its mastery.

When the night comes—comes to lull me to sleep.

And who tells me that the soul, then, does not regret life?

Wednesday 23rd?

ALLAIN—It is almost finished. He is already mad—it is very powerful.

Thursday

Nightmare :

She appeared to me, very beautiful, clothed in an unpleated rochet which fell to her feet like a stole; smiling faintly, she held herself erect, with only her head inclined. A monkey, hopping and skipping, drew nearer; he lifted her mantle, swinging the fringes to and fro. I was afraid to look; I wanted to turn my eyes away but, in spite of myself, I watched.

Under her dress there was nothing; it was black, black as a hole; I wept in despair. Then with both hands she grasped the hem of her dress and threw it over her face. She turned herself inside out like a sack. And I saw nothing more; darkness enveloped her . . . .

I was so frightened that I woke up; the night was so black that I did not know whether it was still the night of my dream.

And then desires become depraved; what happens is very strange : the flesh is listless, indifferent; only the spirit is led astray, but impetuously . . . and what can be done?

Incensed visions appear, supernaturally perverse; enticing chimeras, too unreal for the body; insurmountable disgust for familiar caresses profaned by the lust of the body. Visions of feminine flesh, once evoked to the point of exhaustion—if they appeared now, I would not know what to do with them! The sad part is that the soul is also sullied by this dream of monstrous delights.

O God, having once entertained lofty aspirations, how you grovel now!

Yes, vanity, chastity! Vanity—pride in disguise; thinking oneself superior, towering above others; thinking chastity can be ignored . . . .

. . . Even if it could : but nothing can be suppressed; as soon as he is hemmed in, the Evil One changes his shape; like Proteus he assumes multiple forms, each of which must be subdued separately—quickly he offers still more subtle, more specious delights and holds out the tempting prospect of still more cunning means of satisfying the lusts of the flesh. —Depraved continence! Like perversity, it is its own danger! —O Lord! Protect me from blasphemy.

It is also fortunate that the passions war against one another; —this passion, the worst, oh the passion of Origen, fortunately is contained by pride . . . .

Yes, vanity, chastity!

Be silent, my soul!
Am I to blame, afterwards, if God betrays me?—
But I am not certain; it was beautiful.

. . . An angel came and wrestled with Jacob until the breaking of the day. And when he saw that he could not overcome him, this angel touched the hollow of Jacob's thigh; and the hollow was out of joint as Jacob struggled. The angel said: 'Let me go, for the day is breaking.' And Jacob replied: 'I will not let you go unless you bless me.' The angel said: 'What is your name?' He answered: 'Jacob.'

Then the angel said: 'Your name shall no longer be Jacob, but Israel, for you have struggled with God and are the VICTOR.' Jacob asked him: 'What is your name? Please tell me.' He answered: 'Why do you ask me my name?' And he blessed him.

Jacob called the name of the place Peniel, which means Face of God, *saying: 'I have seen God face to face, and my life is preserved.'*

The sun rose as he passed over Peniel.

That's it, that's the answer.

An angel came and wrestled with Jacob until the breaking of the day . . . . Yes, the end begins to take shape, especially since winter is here and it was snowing only recently;—the white snow in the moonlight almost enticed me. —One supreme night desire maddens him; bewildered, with no prayers in his soul, no longer knowing what to do, he goes out into the night for a walk; the snow on the ground is white. No one knows what he did— but the next day his half-naked body is found lying in the snow . . . .

When I was a child, I wrote :

'. . . maybe I could plunge into the deep snow and find in this icy contact an extraordinary thrill.'

. . . The white mantle that you reserve for the angels . . . .

For he who is dead is free from sin.

And since a moral precept is mandatory, I shall say :

Let the dead bury the dead.

Oh ! Scatter on the living the painful affection which overflows your soul; don't try to find more subtle communions and more gentle signs of tenderness beyond death; there is no sadder illusion . . . then no moral precept is necessary.

Sunday

I am the victor : Lord ! Bless me.[12]

Allain is mad—I am not yet mad—

At least I shall have offered up prayers even after completion of my task, Lord; I am going to be able to rest. —I am very tired . . . .

It is probably autumn; in the evening; a bright fire and lamplight. Familiar looks when eyes are raised, smiles. And you come

---

[12] Gide later remarked that whether he was the victor or the vanquished in the struggle explored in the *Notebooks* was of little importance, that the struggle was itself futile, and that he soon learned the wisdom of surrender.

from time to time to lean over my shoulder and read.

A strange calm, like a beginning of eternity.

And you will find rest for your souls.

Oh! There you are dear soul![13]

I have waited for you a long time . . . .

Do you not know that we shall judge the angels? (St Paul)

Who said that autumn had come? —But it is true, the snow is falling! —What day is it? —How time has passed! —I have difficulty in understanding—too bad! Trying to understand wears me out.

They came close to my bed—I am not sure how many—and talked so loud that my head throbbed. They were saying : 'He has to sleep; no light; turn out all the lights.' Then, to make me sleep, they removed all the sentences from my head; I must have slept for a long time.

. . . For example, it was good to have Emmanuèle there beside me all the time, watching over me and even giving me water. At first I did not recognize her—strange as it seems! I thought that she was dead; we both laughed when I told her about it—

Now she has left me alone; she is in the next room; I get up quietly; she must not hear me—she would come and prevent me from writing : they told me I could not write : —that is why they took away my sentences. —They used them to make a big fire in the room—it was cold!

How white the snow is! —I try to count the flakes, but that takes too long; —the earth is completely white—how beautiful! I remember : yesterday, Emmanuèle took some snow and put it on my forehead—but it all melted . . . . How good it would be to sleep there—it is cool; —it is supposed to be conducive to pleasant dreams. The snow is pure.

---

[13] This page must have been written on the 28th or 29th October. Brain fever, which caused our friend's death, broke out soon afterwards. An interval of three weeks separates these lines from the following, the last written by André Walter. (Gide's note.)

www.ingramcontent.com/pod-product-compliance
Lightning Source LLC
Chambersburg PA
CBHW030521260626
47157CB00005B/1838